# MacLAREN'S MEMORY

## Mara Fitzcharles

## A KISMET® Romance

## METEOR PUBLISHING CORPORATION
### Bensalem, Pennsylvania

To Terry for her enduring friendship
   and
To my husband for his love and his patience.

**MARA FITZCHARLES**

Born, raised, and educated in eastern Pennsylvania, Mara Fitzcharles now lives in northeastern Maryland, not quite deep enough in the woods or close enough to the water to satisfy her love of nature. In addition to reading and writing, she enjoys long walks, classical music, and traveling throughout the United States with her husband and four sons.

# ONE

Brianna thought her legs were going to crumble beneath her as she crossed the wide lobby and headed toward the tinted glass doors that opened onto the busy street. With each successive step the weakness increased, the wobbly feeling became more evident.

She passed the last row of little shops lining the concourse without so much as a sideward glance. Her fingers tightened round her packages. She drew in a deep breath and concentrated all her efforts on the simple task of walking as she made her way to the door that somehow seemed miles away, instead of mere feet in front of her.

Brianna shifted her shopping bags and pushed her shoulder against the glass. As the door swung open, she stepped into sunlight, intensely bright after the artificial light inside.

The blazing midday heat still poured from the sidewalk and, trapped by the tall buildings, made the late afternoon air oppressive. The humidity hit her full force, like a blanket smothering her with its weight.

She felt herself swoon; then all at once, everything went black. She reached out, instinctively grabbing for something to hold on to, but her arm sliced through the muggy air. And as the veil of unconsciousness slipped over her, she sank toward the pavement.

His voice penetrated the cloak of darkness weighing her down. Jess's voice. Low, rumbling, and sensuous. It was calling her, begging her to wake up. Although his voice was familiar, the urgency was not.

At first she fought against his repeated summons, wanting to remain cocooned in the peaceful, dreamlike state. She lay contentedly against his chest, listening to his heartbeat, breathing in the scent that was uniquely his, and wondering why he sounded so concerned. She was accustomed to commanding, to playful, to loving. . . . But not concerned.

He spoke again, drawing her, little by little, into the realm of awareness. Soon other voices became evident in the background. Hushed voices. And then sounds of traffic. Horns blaring. Tires humming on the street.

Once more Jess repeated his gentle command to wake up. She struggled to see through the heavy haze of darkness. She breathed in deeply, slowly filling her lungs with much needed air.

Why were there horns blaring? Why was that edge of concern in Jess's voice?

*Jess*?

She groaned. Then, with great effort, she willed herself out from the darkness, forced her eyelids to lift. . . .

The sunlight was blinding. She shut her eyes swiftly

and turned her head into the nubby fabric of Jess's jacket.

*Jess's jacket?* That was impossible. Jess had been gone from her life for five years. And he'd never worn a jacket. His normal attire had been a pair of jogging shorts, nothing more.

"Wake up. Come on. Wake up," his velvet-edged voice coaxed.

*Jess's voice. Jess's scent.*

She dared to open her eyes again.

*Jess's face.* Sunlight glinting in his thick auburn hair. Warm malachite eyes staring into hers. Jess's eyes.

Her reaction was as much second nature as breathing. She slid her hand around his neck, pulled his head toward her, and kissed him.

The heat of their kiss was intense, but oh so sweet. . . . It had been too long. . . . She hungered for the taste of him. He had always tasted of spearmint. As she pressed her lips against his mouth, she realized he still did.

Although she had initiated the kiss, she felt him respond, felt his warm lips assume control and then possess her mouth with remembered mastery, driving her toward the brink of passion.

Brianna sensed more than felt his sterling self-control struggling to surface and eased away from the intimacy of their kiss. She leaned back onto the muscled arm that cradled her and sighed happily.

"That was some kiss, blue eyes," he observed.

The familiar endearment falling so naturally from his lips pleased her and she smiled in satisfaction. Her thumb traced the edge of the slim band of silver circling her ring finger.

"What happened?" she asked, staring up at his beloved face.

"You fainted," he explained. His eyes twinkled with amusement while, at the same time, one eyebrow rose curiously.

"That's not what I meant," Brianna murmured. But she was too shaky and weak to bother explaining what she did mean. Her eyelids shuttered closed again. "I should have eaten."

"All right, folks," he announced to the crowd milling about. "Show's over. She's okay. She missed a meal."

"Two," Brianna admitted, remembering how eager she'd been earlier to explore as much of Boston as she could.

"Two? You missed two meals?"

She levered herself up from her prone position. "Hmm," she confessed, nodding twice in response.

"I suppose you'd better eat before you do anything else." Encircling her waist, he lifted her to her feet. "Come on. I'm on my way to dinner. I don't want to be late."

The crowd of onlookers began to disperse. Brianna smiled awkwardly at the few stragglers who remained. She hated being on display. The secure feeling of Jess's large hand gently gripping her arm drew her back to him.

"Feeling better?" he asked.

"Better than what?"

He didn't bother to suppress his amusement. He shook his head, then pursed his lips. "Better than you look. You're white as a ghost."

"It figures," she muttered. "I feel kind of spooky . . . shaky . . . a little disoriented."

"We'll take it slow and easy," he assured her.

She made an attempt to straighten her sash and brush off her thin gauze skirt, but the fabric clung to her. She was unpleasantly sticky and damp. And she felt hot, too, not simply from their kiss or the unseasonably warm weather. His hand, wrapped around her upper arm, fueled the inner heat their kiss had sparked.

She was not surprised by her body's response. His touch had always warmed her like this, as if an invisible electric current was shooting through her. And the brush of his lips against hers had been incendiary. The kiss they'd just shared had fallen a bit short of those she remembered so well. Of course, this was a public place. Jess had seldom kissed her properly in public.

She accepted the fact that today was different. They hadn't been together for a long, long while. At first he'd responded as eagerly as always. But then, she'd sensed his reserve and knew he was holding back.

Brianna tucked a wayward strand of hair behind her ear and squared her small shoulders. For five years she had missed him, longed for him, loved him. For five years she had wondered about him. And now, by some odd quirk of fate, she'd stumbled, literally, into his path.

As soon as she shook the aftereffects of the dizziness and managed to gather her wits about her, she intended to seek answers to the endless stream of questions spanning the years. But for now, she would cope with the lingering weakness that didn't feel much like the results of a forgotten meal. For now she accepted his comforting presence as divine intervention.

She raised her head and found him staring, his eyes filled with a puzzling mixture of interest and concern.

"Your eyes are beautiful," he murmured unexpectedly. For a fleeting moment he looked as if he'd surprised himself by voicing his thoughts.

She stepped away slightly, taken aback by the sudden compliment, but more by his tone. His voice quavered with the same gentle reverence it had when they'd made love. She swallowed hard, denying the memories that gentle, sexy rumble evoked. Then, calling upon her inner strength to see her through, she bent to retrieve her fallen packages.

"Don't bother. I'll carry those," he insisted. "I suspect you're not too steady on your feet."

She watched as he tucked the shopping bags under his arm. He had always been in control. Today was no different. When he slid his fingers beneath her elbow, cupping it in his free hand, she didn't protest. When he moved forward, she just naturally followed his lead.

"My car isn't far from here," he said, guiding her away from the building. "Let's go."

She did her best to keep up with him, which was no easy task. He was tall, over six feet in comparison to her five foot almost one inch. And he was lean and well muscled. His fast pace and long strides had often been a challenge to her. Now, it seemed, he tempered his normal tendency in deference to her size and circumstance.

"I suppose I ought to introduce myself," he said. "Mom always taught my sisters not to get into a car with a stranger. I'm Mac—"

"Mac?" Brianna echoed, interrupting him. Surprise and confusion overwhelmed her at the same time.

"Right. And you are?"

"Brianna Dugan." It was a conditioned response. Her name tumbled forth politely. Her thoughts moved swiftly on to another place. And while she fought her way through the fog of bewilderment, he kept talking.

"Pleased to meet you, Ms. Dugan. Although I suspect this introduction is a tad unconventional, I admit I'm flattered to have had such a lovely lady falling at my feet. Normally if someone on the street tries that hard to get your attention, they're looking for a handout."

"I'm not—" she began.

"I know," he said, winking at her. "Panhandlers don't carry bags of loot from exclusive little shops."

"Souvenirs," she explained quietly.

"Ah, Celtic shirts, no doubt."

"No. Not a one."

"My mistake," he conceded as they came to an abrupt halt next to a sleek silver Corvette.

Her eyes raced from the car to the man and back again. Confusion hammered her walls of reason. He *looked* like Jess. He *sounded* like Jess. He even smelled and tasted like Jess. But he said his name was *Mac*.

And he drove a Corvette. Jess had driven a battered old jeep. Dented. With blotches of touch-up paint decorating the exterior and patches covering the torn seats inside. His lifestyle had definitely not included Corvettes. He had eaten from a hodgepodge of tacky plastic dishes—the dime store variety. And he'd lived in a tiny furnished apartment, no bigger than a postage stamp— hundreds of miles away from Boston. . . .

As he held the car door open, she stole one last reassuring look. *Mac?* she thought. *No way. This is Jess. No one else could possibly have that distinctive cowlick and that relaxed air of authority. But he's treating me as if I'm a stranger. . . . That just isn't possi-*

*ble, not after what we shared. . . . Something's wrong
. . . something more than my confusion.*

She allowed him to help her into the car, but her
movements were mechanical. Her mind raced onward—
tripping through long corridors of memories whose
doors had been closed for years.

The car horn blared as he pulled into traffic, and
Brianna flinched. She turned to face him, immediately
realizing what a mistake that movement was. The seats
were practically on top of one another and the effect
his closeness had on her was hard to deny.

She felt woozy again, as she had when that blast of
warm air had hit her. Yet different somehow. This feeling wasn't a physical reaction to heat or hunger. It was
an emotional response to him.

"Put your head between your knees," he advised.
"It's supposed to help."

She did as he instructed. The feeling passed.

"How did you know I wasn't feeling well?" she
asked, resting her head back against the car seat.

"I caught a glimpse of you out of the corner of my
eye. You were white as a sheet."

"I'm staying at the Sheraton," she began.

"Dinner is our first stop," he contradicted, his tone
firm and decisive.

"But—" she tried to protest.

"No buts," he insisted. "You need to eat."

She closed her eyes. Her thumb rubbed against the
edge of her ring. The gesture was reassuring. She'd
often lost to Jess in the struggle of wills. And it had
never bothered her. She'd loved him. He'd loved her.
There had been plenty of sharing, plenty of give and
take in their relationship. She wouldn't argue with him.
She didn't feel up to it.

"Am I allowed one question?" Brianna dared to ask.

She heard his familiar laughter. It started low and rumbled slowly in his chest before bursting forth.

"You can ask me as many questions as you like, blue eyes," he informed her.

Brianna's eyes flew open instantly. That was the second time he'd used the once-familiar nickname. "Excuse me?" she whispered.

"Ask away," he said. "But don't get too personal. We just met, after all."

She studied his face intently, wondering about him. One moment she was certain he was Jess, calling her "blue eyes" as he had so many times before. The next moment, he was a stranger, reminding her they'd just met.

"Where are you taking me?" Brianna asked, her soft voice weighted with determination. In her own way, she was demanding an explanation and letting him know she wouldn't meekly agree to go along with him unless she chose to do so.

"Home," he responded easily. "Well, to my parent's home. It's Sunday. My family always has dinner together on Sunday. Don't worry. You'll be welcome."

"I don't believe this," she breathed.

"Relax. You need to eat. It's a simple family dinner."

"Dinner at my house was never simple," she muttered.

"No?"

"No. My mother was a perfectionist. She never allowed uninvited guests."

"Mom loves company. She wouldn't complain if each of us showed up with an extra."

"Each?" Brianna repeated. "How many of you are there?"

"I'm the oldest of six. Four boys. Two girls."

He sounded as though he was bragging. She closed her eyes again. *What have I gotten myself into?* she questioned silently.

"Are you all right?"

"Fine," she assured him. The doors to the halls of memory flung wide open again. Jess had mentioned his brothers on occasion—rare occasion. They'd been completely wrapped up in the present, in each other, in sharing as much as they could emotionally and physically. They hadn't talked of past or future. There hadn't been a need to discuss family or friends, just a constant need for each other. She tried to force the doors closed.

"No more questions?" His deep voice held a teasing note. One Brianna was sure she recognized.

*Plenty more. But where do I start?* she wondered.

She chose to keep the conversation light. This was not the place for heavy conversation. Only a fool would attempt anything serious while sitting in the middle of Boston's traffic. And until she felt better, there was no use discussing anything of importance.

"Does everyone come home for Sunday dinner?" she asked.

"Whenever possible. Everyone's expected to be there this evening. Luke, who's two years younger than I am, is always home for meals. He has a connecting studio apartment. He's an architect. Inherited the artistic genes passed on through the last few generations from my great-grandfather, who designed and constructed some magnificent sailing vessels. Luke's easygoing. You'll like him.

"Number three son is Andrew. He's fifteen months

younger than Luke. Drew is our crusader and our rebel. He has a degree in engineering and a pilot's license. For the last few years he's been employed by an organization that provides food to starving communities worldwide. Many of these places are experiencing political unrest. Drew thrives on adventure and involvement. He's much more brash and opinionated than Luke, but I don't think he'll be difficult in your presence."

She nodded, acknowledging his comments as he rambled on. She couldn't keep her eyes from straying to his bold profile. She admired his unmistakable self-assurance. She always had. He had been confident and outgoing while she had always been reserved and private.

Brianna smiled to herself as she listened to him talk. Even though he'd introduced himself as Mac, he possessed every one of the traits she'd admired in Jess, plus a few she'd merely accepted as part of him. Jess had a tendency to expound on subjects, like colonial history, which were dear to his heart. She realized from his present monologue he had not changed.

"My sister Sara is married to her high school sweetheart, Ted. Sara has her share of the artistic genes also but, thankfully, not the temperament. She's extremely personable, effervescent, and," he cleared his throat, "pregnant. They're expecting their first child.

"Rachel is next in line." He paused and shook his head. "Rachel celebrated her twenty-first birthday last month, but then, Rachel's whole life is a celebration. She's the most outgoing member of the family. If you initiate a conversation with her, you'll never forget it. She talks perpetually!

"The youngest is Ethan. He's . . . charming, yet headstrong. Truly received his share of artistic ability and temperament from old Grandpa Jonas. He's the ladies' man of the family, but don't let him turn your head," he advised, winking in her direction.

Brianna smiled graciously, but as she listened, she grew uneasy. She realized meeting a large family under normal circumstances would be challenging for her. But today was far from normal. She'd just run smack into a man she hadn't seen for five years—a lover who had not acknowledged he even knew her. On top of that, she was feeling increasingly tired.

"Dad owns a shipbuilding business that's been our family's livelihood for over one hundred years," he continued. "Ask him one question about his 'pride and joy' and he'll regale you with chapters of history.

"Mom is intelligent, well-read, soft-spoken, completely devoted to our family and our home, but involved in church and community as well. I've yet to meet anyone who didn't get along famously with her.

"In addition to my parents and siblings, my sister Sara's husband, Ted, and my gal, Chris, will be there," he continued, "as will Rand and Tessa. . . ."

Brianna was aware he was still speaking, but she heard nothing after his *gal*. That one simple word convinced her she was wading into deep waters and would soon be in over her head.

"I don't think I can manage a crowd right now," she said, her voice no more than a whisper.

"It isn't a crowd. It's only a large, loving family," he replied rather impatiently.

Brianna bristled at his tone. She turned her head away quickly. Jess had never been impatient. Unexpected tears filled her eyes. She fought to hold them back and won.

"You've told me about your family, but you haven't

told me about yourself. What do you do?'' she questioned, wanting to satisfy her curiosity.

"I'm an attorney. My uncle and I have a family law practice," he replied.

Once more the similarities slammed into Brianna.

"Where did you go to law school?" she ventured as the memory of another place and time assailed her.

He didn't respond.

"Mac?" she persisted.

"I went to law school out of state," he replied tersely. Then, as if to say 'It's none of your business,' he directed the conversation back to her. "Why don't you relax, Brianna? Your color isn't any better than it was back there on the sidewalk. My family won't be a problem. I know you'll be comfortable with them. You might even like them if you try."

"I really don't think this is a good idea," Brianna stressed as she fought another sudden wave of weakness, not unlike the one preceding her fall. She often missed meals when she was working, but skipping a meal had never made her feel like this. She sucked in a large breath of air and released it very slowly.

The faint noise drew his attention. He shot a quick glance in her direction.

"You sound as if you're apprehensive."

"I am."

"It's only a large, loving family," he emphasized.

"I'm a stranger."

"You *will* be welcome," he insisted. "I told you that. However, if you'd prefer, we'll pick up an order of fast food and take it back to my place. Although I honestly believe you're more likely to be comfortable with my family."

Silence was the response. It filled the interior of the

car while the words *my family* echoed through Brianna's head.

When he stopped for a red light, he leaned back in his seat, pushed his long arms straight out against the steering wheel, and turned to face her.

"Would you rather be alone with me or have the company of my family?" he asked, pressing her for a decision.

Bravely she searched his face for some sign of recognition. All she found there was concern. Maybe compassion. But nothing more. No spark of remembrance. No hint of affection. No trace of a love that had forever claimed her heart.

He studied her, too. Although she remained chalky white and appeared exhausted, he couldn't ignore the exquisite, fragile beauty of her features. Her bewitching blue eyes kept him captive when he would have looked away.

For endless seconds he peered into clear, pale eyes that beckoned him like a siren's lure. Something drew him into their enchanting depths. Something vaguely familiar, and regretfully elusive . . .

The car behind him honked loudly and long. He gave the stoplight a cursory glance before he proceeded on his way.

She still had not responded.

"I suppose it's better to err on the side of caution," he said.

"It really doesn't make any difference," Brianna muttered. She didn't care. She felt strange. Weak. It didn't make any difference where or what she ate, as long as it was soon. And she didn't need to err on any side. This man, although he professed to be a stranger, was familiar. She was sure he was Jess. Instinct or sixth sense—*something* made her absolutely certain.

It wasn't possible for one man to look and smell and taste and act so completely like another. It wasn't possible for two different men to have warm malachite eyes that sent currents of sensation through her. It wasn't possible for another man's touch to cause the heat this man's touch caused. And nowhere on earth could there be hair that shade of deep auburn with the distinctive cowlick in the front.

This man who called himself Mac was Jess. She was certain. She'd follow him anywhere without reservation. To his parents' home. To his place. To the proverbial ends of the earth. He wasn't a stranger. And just as soon as she'd eaten and was feeling better, she'd find out exactly what was going on.

Mac glanced toward the passenger seat. His companion had fallen asleep while he'd been trying to concentrate on maneuvering his 'Vette safely through the crowded streets. His family would be shocked. It wasn't unusual for Rachel or Ethan to drag home a stray or bring an unexpected guest to dinner. But no one would expect *him* to walk in with an unannounced guest, much less a stranger. He was the levelheaded, even-tempered, predictable brother.

But Brianna Dugan intrigued him. She puzzled him. In fact, she had bewitched him, probably with that sudden, unexplainable kiss.

His mind wandered while his eyes remained focused on the flow of traffic. He couldn't help wondering why she had kissed him in the first place, although he wouldn't complain. The kiss, while altogether surprising, was sweet and fiery. It hit him with inexplicable force. He could still feel its lingering effects.

Her kiss had touched him. No, it had seized him. He knew he'd responded the instant her soft lips brushed against his. They'd begged silently for more and he'd given more. Mindlessly.

The trouble was, it felt good. Great. So great, he remembered, he'd wanted it to continue. And that was out of the question. They'd been in a very public place. And he was not inclined toward public displays of emotion. Nor was he inclined to casual encounters with strange women.

He smiled at himself then, at his apparent lack of breeding and lack of consideration. He'd been uncharacteristically rude. She'd said she was staying at the Sheraton, but he'd never bothered to ask if she was alone or if someone would be expecting her to return. He hadn't asked why she was in Boston, or where she was from, or what she did. He'd just rambled on and on about his family, without asking about hers. He made a mental note to apologize when she wakened.

And then, he wondered why she had neglected to eat. There were plenty of places mixed in among the shops where she could have had a meal. He knew many women approached shopping with the kind of zeal that had coined the saying "Shop till you drop." But he'd never believed anyone shopped with so much gusto that she actually kept at it until she was physically exhausted. Even now, darting a glance in her direction, he wasn't satisfied that's what had happened.

His smile grew deeper as he remembered his first glimpse of Little Miss Shopper. He'd made a quick stop at his office en route to dinner and was on his way out of the building when he'd spied her. The cascade of rich, sable hair had drawn his attention. Not that he was particularly attracted to dark-haired women; on the contrary, he preferred blondes. But he'd noticed this woman just the same. He had watched her with pure male pleasure as the teal blue skirt swirled around her shapely legs. Then, as he'd admired her petite womanly body, he'd become aware those same shapely legs were unsteady. Although she was toting several shopping bags, he didn't think they were heavy enough to burden her.

He'd quickened his pace as she neared the door, not knowing what motivated him more, his customary good manners or a peculiar niggling concern that seemed to make its presence felt as he watched her progress. Just as he reached her, she started to sink.

From that point, his movements had been reflexive. He'd caught her to break the fall, gathered her into his arms, and crouched down to cushion her limp form on his legs. He'd been oblivious to the gathering crowd, for the most part.

She weighed no more than a whisper lying across his lap. And the feel of her body against his own created surprising and unexpected reactions. The strongest felt like need, as if his flesh were intentionally reacting to hers, communicating a powerful, instinctive need to touch. He'd drawn her more securely into his arms.

As he'd crooned quietly in an effort to revive her, he stared, blatantly, at her face. Tiny, delicate features formed out of creamy white, porcelain-smooth skin. Yet unlike porcelain, she was soft and her skin was warm. It begged to be touched.

While his thumb strayed to the underside of her chin, he'd stopped himself just short of tracing the bow of her lips with his index finger.

When she'd finally lifted her lacy, dark eyelashes, he found himself peering into the palest blue eyes imaginable. Crystal clear, azure blue—like the sparkling eyes that ran through his dreams. Except these eyes were not sparkling; they were clouded by confusion.

Perhaps it was the confusion that drew his response. More likely it was the feeling that tightened his gut when she'd looked up at him. That feeling intensified when she'd placed her lips so gently over his and then communicated her need so convincingly with her mouth. And when she had finally spoken, the softness of her voice somehow conveyed more than her words.

His polite concern had swiftly, surely changed to involvement. It was then his awareness of the crowd circling them had become acute. He wanted them gone. And he wasted no time telling them so.

The rest had come easily. He'd taken over, assumed control, as he always did. He was on his way to dinner. She needed to eat. It was as simple as that. He escorted her to his car and here they were.

Brianna was dreaming. Waves pounded the shore, then tripped away. Jess's arm around her waist held her tightly against his lean body. Moonlight shadowed his face and the warmth of his breath caressed her. He was smiling, and she shared the satisfaction his smile implied.

Their rare evening together had been wonderful. Special. He'd begged her to meet him at dusk. And when she'd arrived, he'd had a twilight picnic prepared for her there on the beach. It wasn't much. Crackers, cheese, goose liver pâté—a favorite of his—two pears, and one lovely, long-stemmed rose—for her. He'd kissed her, repeatedly, and promised her champagne the next time. . . .

She felt his lips on hers, his hands on her body as they embraced. . . .

And then she heard his voice from far away. She didn't want him to talk. She wanted him to kiss her again. She wanted him to make love to her again. She wanted Jess . . .

Jess.

Brianna opened her eyes slowly as she came awake. She remembered she was in Boston. In a car with a man who said his name was Mac.

"We're almost there," he told her quietly. "That's why I woke you. I thought you might want a few minutes to chase the sleep from your eyes."

"Thanks," she murmured, casting a worried glance in his direction. "I'm still not sure I like this."

"I know," he replied, his deep voice filled with concern. "I understand your reluctance, believe me. Why don't you allow me to make the decision—"

"You already have."

"Yes, I have. I suspect you're battling more than hunger."

"Hmm," she conceded. "Maybe I am."

She knew very well she was dealing with more than hunger. She was confused by her companion's lack of recognition. Her mind felt fuzzy and muddled as she struggled to put the puzzle of memory versus reality together. And beyond that, she was battling an undeniable fatigue that had crept up and slipped over her. But she refused to succumb to it.

On the surface she appeared delicate, even fragile. In fact, she was not. While she possessed an amazing calm that quite accurately reflected the deep, still waters of her personality, hidden beneath the surface lay reservoirs of self-reliance and determination. They ran deep and continually fueled her, providing her with tremendous inner strength, the core of her surface poise. She was a wellspring of serenity. And that serenity only added to her demeanor of fragility.

She glanced briefly at the man driving the car. The sight of that familiar profile tugged on her heartstrings and she suppressed the urge to reach toward him. Instead she forced herself to turn away, staring out the window at the scenery beyond the confines of the Corvette.

They were passing through an old, established neighborhood. On either side of the tree-lined streets were large rambling homes, mostly Victorian, with perfectly manicured lawns and gardens. The neighborhood screamed old money. And it fit the present image of the car's immaculately groomed driver, but not her memory of Jess.

When the car slowed, then turned into a long, narrow driveway leading to one of these stately houses, she was not surprised. But she was puzzled.

# _____ TWO _____

Towering pine trees rose along the winding road, obscuring Brianna's view of the house and the grounds. She had only a glimpse of the huge structure through the trees before the car stopped. It was, in a word, imposing. Not unlike the man seated beside her.

While she craned her neck to stare out the window at the magnificent facade, he came around to her side of the car.

"You know, Mom's remedy for most anything is a tall glass of cold milk," he informed her as he opened the door. "She always offers milk when either of my sisters feels light-headed. And she swears it's the reason her girls have such beautiful skin and her boys are all so tall. Never mind genetics."

He laughed then. The rich, warm sound brought Brianna's eyes abruptly to his face.

"While I'm certain it's not the cure-all Mom believes it to be," he continued, "I think you ought to indulge yourself as soon as we're inside. It couldn't hurt, could it?'' he inquired, peering down at her.

Brianna felt helpless. She gazed into those familiar eyes and could not manage even a simple response.

She soon realized she was not alone. He stared at her, long and hard, with a peculiar look on his face she did not recognize or understand.

Finally he spoke. But his low voice was quiet, his speech slow and distinct. ''Drink to me only with thine eyes,'' he recited reverently.

''And I will pledge with mine,'' she responded.

''You're familiar with Jonson.''

She nodded, still watching him.

''It somehow seemed appropriate,'' he explained, shrugging apologetically.

Brianna nodded again. ''*To Celia.* I've heard it many times—''

''Must be your eyes,'' he interrupted.

Those eyes, filled to overflowing with unanswered questions, assessed him thoughtfully.

Jess had often called her ''blue eyes''. And he had frequently quoted Jonson or Lord Byron's *She Walks in Beauty*. He hadn't dwelled upon her appearance, but at odd moments he had bestowed lofty compliments on her, telling her he couldn't afford to give her beautiful gifts, only beautiful borrowed words. And always he'd promised her more in the future. ''Someday, blue eyes, I'll bring you champagne and roses.'' Or ''Someday, blue eyes, this will be Limoges, not tacky plastic.''

Brianna had never needed his promises. She'd only wanted him. She had never weaved dreams, she'd lived reality. Jess had been her reality. Her world had revolved around him.

That same world now tilted on its axis. And not

merely because of her confusion. She was surprisingly shaky, feeling the aftereffects of her dizzy spell. So she allowed herself to be led up the steps, relying on his strength to keep her upright.

As they stepped into the wide foyer, they were greeted by the sound of lilting laughter. And he had barely finished closing the heavy door behind them when a smiling auburn-haired beauty stood, wide-eyed, before them.

In a glance Brianna realized the woman was one of his sisters. Her hair was the same remarkable shade of deep auburn as his. She was a tall, very feminine version of him, unmistakably beautiful and obviously pregnant.

"Well, hello," she said, eyeing the two of them thoroughly. "You're late! Such bad manners. But you've brought a guest, so you're forgiven." She smiled warmly at Brianna. "I'm Sara O'Roarke. Please come in and make yourself comfortable."

With an elegant sweep of her hand, she welcomed Brianna, but Sara's emerald eyes flashed curiously toward her brother.

"This is Brianna Dugan," he hastened to explain, knowing full well Sara expected an explanation. "I stopped at the office, then ducked into one of those little shops to buy a card for Rand. As I was leaving I ran into Brianna trying to sweep the pavement."

His sister's eyebrows rose.

"Literally," Brianna confirmed. "I fainted."

"At my feet," he chimed in. "I caught her in the nick of time."

Sara's smile faded instantly and her look changed to one of concern. "Well, for heaven's sake. Come sit down. How are you feeling now?"

"She hasn't eaten," Mac answered for her. As his eyes met Sara's, brother and sister grinned identical grins and, in unison, said, "Milk."

"Would you mind?" he asked.

"Not at all. Why don't you go sit down and I'll be right back with Mom's cure-all," Sara agreed, calling over her shoulder as she took off down the hallway in the other direction.

He winked at Brianna. The confident smile on his face seemed to say "I told you so."

"I'm not the only one who's been brainwashed by Mom," he said, his eyes lit with good humor. "Let's join the others while Sara's getting the cure."

Brianna stepped in front of him as he motioned her toward the doorway. Before they progressed five feet into the large living room, they were stopped by another redheaded sister. This one wore her long, straight hair worked into a loose braid flopped casually over her shoulder. She was only a few inches taller than Brianna.

"Oh hi, Mac. We wondered where you were. Chris thought maybe you'd misunderstood her and driven out to pick her up instead of meeting her here. And you were so late. That's just not like you. I started worrying you'd been in another accident and Ethan said it was too early to call out a search and rescue team—"

"Slow down, Rachel," he broke in. "I apologize for my tardiness. I didn't mean to upset you. If you'll allow me a moment to speak, I'll introduce you to my excuse—Brianna Dugan. Brianna, my sister Rachel."

Brianna smiled at the gregarious redhead facing her. She most definitely was not as poised as Sara. Her welcoming hand trembled. And when Brianna met her lovely green eyes, she thought she saw a hint of anxiety.

"Are you—the author of *A Lonely Road*?" Rachel asked.

Brianna nodded, releasing Rachel's hand as she did.

"Really?" Rachel raced onward, not giving her a chance to reply. "When I started reading it, I got so choked up midway through I had to put it aside for a while. You express feelings so powerfully. It took me days to talk myself into finishing it."

"Thank you, Rachel," she replied. "It is sad in a few places. But life can be that way."

"I thought you were going to let Brianna sit down," Sara scolded as she approached them, milk in hand. She gently nudged her brother out of the way and, placing a slender hand around Brianna's wrist, pulled her toward the overstuffed plaid couch. "Please sit down," Sara urged. The look in her eyes directed Brianna to seat herself immediately.

"You'd probably be wise to drink this milk as soon as possible. If Mom finds out you haven't, we'll both get lectured," she said, dropping onto the cushion beside Brianna. "She's in the kitchen, but she promised to join us shortly."

"Rachel accosted us before we made it two feet into the room," Mac explained.

"I don't know why you're blaming me, big brother," Rachel countered. "You have to admit it's unusual for you to bring anyone extra for dinner. I was curious, and not without justification. Sara, you read *A Lonely Road*, didn't you?"

"That's why your name sounded familiar," Sara realized suddenly. "I knew I'd heard it, but I couldn't remember where. I do remember discussing your book with Mom, though. We decided you handled a difficult topic with extreme sensitivity. Motherhood is challenging enough,'' Sara emphasized. ''But without a helpmate? It must be nigh unto impossible! I can't imagine having this baby without Ted by my side.''

''Lots of things seem easier if we have someone beside us, holding our hand,'' Brianna agreed. As a knot of anxiety tightened her stomach, she glanced toward Mac to see if he was listening.

She saw a tall, willowy blonde kiss him lightly on the cheek, then link her arm through his possessively as she greeted him. She did not hear what the blonde said.

As if he felt the weight of her stare, Mac turned to face Brianna and politely introduced her to the newcomer. ''Brianna, this is Chris Whitney.''

With a slight rise of her brows, the blonde seemed to wait for him to say more. Then she turned to Brianna and smiled warmly. ''Mac tends to introduce me as though we're only friends. There are some things you just can't change in a man, aren't there?''

Brianna was grateful to have the couch beneath her as she nodded her head and murmured, ''Pleased to meet you.'' But nothing cushioned the impact of Chris's words. The meaning was clear. Watching as he slipped a sheltering arm around Chris added to her confusion and heaped new hurt on top of old wounds.

Her thumb pressed against the ring on her left hand. Images of Jess lying next to her, whispering to her, telling her he loved her, blurred Brianna's vision. She inhaled deeply and squared her shoulders, realizing she had unconsciously plastered the same pleasant smile on her face she often wore for strangers. It was the one she wore while signing autographs, facing nameless people, and wishing she were hidden away at home with those she loved.

"Make sure you finish that milk before Mom appears," Sara advised.

"I'll do my best," Brianna returned, grateful for the distraction. She found she was equally grateful when Sara offered an explanation for her unexpected presence. Brianna didn't want to think about the beautiful blonde, much less converse with the woman. Her thoughts centered on Jess.

As conversation moved forth around her, she realized she ought to pay attention to what was being said. She struggled to pull her thoughts into the present, aware that this large room was filled with *his* family, *his* loved ones.

When she raised her head, her eyes automatically sought him out. He was leaning toward Chris, whispering something private in her ear, dropping a kiss on her temple. Brianna winced and quickly looked away, choosing to focus her attention on her surroundings.

The room wasn't at all what she expected. Before she'd come inside, she had an impression of wealth, yet this room smacked of home. It was attractively decorated, but for comfort, not for show.

This wasn't a room to admire, it was a room that was used. Sara had curled her feet beneath her on the big plaid couch and rested her head upon a hand-embroidered pillow. Magazines were stacked haphazardly next to a tray of fresh vegetables on the coffee table. And there were photos everywhere—lovingly, proudly displayed family photographs.

While the furnishings may have been expensive, they'd been selected to create a warm, welcoming atmosphere. If wealth lived here, it was sublimely understated.

Brianna's eyes strayed to the far corner of the room and the massive stone fireplace. She watched as the animated red-haired man sitting on the hearth gestured to the couple talking with him. His hair was typically carrot red, like Rachel's, and his merry green eyes were like Mac's.

There was a striking family resemblance. She'd seen it in his sisters, but now she saw the likeness in a male face as well. And in each, male and female, she found green eyes so similar they made her too-fuzzy head spin more.

Smiling green eyes, laughing green eyes. Perfect likenesses of those she was so familiar with.

*His* family.

She felt an odd tug of sadness. Years before she'd hoped to share a home and family with Jess. She'd thought he'd wanted to share that with her, too. She'd been sure of it when he'd slipped the sparkling diamond on her finger. And then, he'd disappeared. He hadn't met her as he'd promised.

She'd waited for him on the beach, as always. She'd returned day after day for weeks. She'd even gone to his apartment several times—but he was gone.

She hadn't known where or why. He'd simply vanished from her life. No explanation. Nothing. He'd promised, as he always did, "See you tomorrow, Bri!" But that promise had not been fulfilled. All the following tomorrows Brianna had been alone. . . .

Then today this man had introduced himself as Mac. . . .

Mac? Through the fog of confusion clouding her

mind, Brianna made the connection. And seconds later her certainty of that knowledge was confirmed.

From the doorway a loud voice boomed, "Jess MacLaren, I'm ashamed of you! You haven't bothered to introduce me to our guest!"

Brianna flinched, not from the volume of the man's voice, but from the name he spoke. Jess MacLaren. *Her* Jess.

Mac *was* Jess.

As the reality sank in, she felt a wave of disconcerting emotion wash over her. The milk glass almost slipped from her hand. Thankfully, her hard-won serenity came to her aid before its contents did little more than slosh slightly over the rim.

"Whoa, Dad. Take it easy. You scared our guest." The low, rumbling voice, not unlike Jess's, was close by. It belonged to the man who'd just seated himself alongside her.

"You okay?" he asked.

Brianna nodded.

"I'm Luke," the man said.

"Dad, allow me to introduce Brianna Dugan," Mac interrupted, his voice every bit as commanding as his father's. "Brianna, the big guy with the equally big mouth is my father, Jonas MacLaren." Mac's manner was both easy and relaxed as he performed the necessary introduction and indirectly kidded his father in the process.

She responded with a polite, "I'm pleased to meet you, Mr. MacLaren." She even managed to keep her proper smile in place as Jonas MacLaren shook her hand and welcomed her to his home.

Her busy eyes darted back and forth from the father to his son, Jess. *Her* Jess.

Brianna's confusion was not well disguised.

"We are a bit overwhelming all at once, aren't we?" Luke observed.

She turned toward the deep, rumbling voice, coming almost face to face with the man seated beside her.

"More than just a bit to me," she responded candidly. "I'm afraid I'm not very adept in situations like this." As she spoke she studied him. He was tall, with the same lean, muscular build as Jess and similar eyes. But this man's hair was darker, more chestnut-colored than red, and he had a mustache.

"You have no reason to apologize," he told her. "Mac has a take-charge quality. He doesn't always consider all sides before he makes a decision. Not that he's impulsive. He's not. He just does what he feels is right and expects everyone to agree."

"I've noticed," she murmured.

"You sure you're all right?" Luke asked again.

Brianna felt the light touch of Sara's hand on her knee and turned toward her. "Are you feeling faint again?" Sara inquired softly. "Perhaps you ought to lie down for a while."

"Perhaps I should," Brianna agreed. Her head was spinning, but from confusion, not dizziness. Mac was Jess. He was not a stranger. He'd been her lover. And more . . .

"Come on," Sara said, rising to her feet gracefully in spite of her bulging figure. "I'll show you to my old room."

As Luke pushed the bedroom door open, it creaked on its hinges. Sara's room was dark, except for a soft light from the small lamp on the desk in the alcove.

"Jess?" Brianna murmured weakly.

Luke paused momentarily, then ambled over to Sara's four-poster and plunked himself down on the high mattress.

Drowsy blue eyes searched his face.

"Where's Jess?"

"In the living room saying good-bye to Chris. You're stuck with me for the time being. How're you feeling?"

"Lousy."

"Can I get you anything?"

Brianna shook her head and allowed her heavy eyelids to droop closed.

He studied her in silence, trying to make a decision. She'd called out his brother's name before she was fully awake. But she'd called him Jess, not Mac. And that puzzled him.

"Are you still with me?" he asked quietly. He'd made his decision. Nothing ventured, nothing gained.

Brianna made a feeble attempt to nod.

"Mind if I ask you a question?"

Slowly she opened her bleary eyes, focusing with difficulty on Luke.

"You knew my brother before today, didn't you?" he charged.

Her mouth dropped open. She almost gasped, but again her normal serenity, shaken though it was, carried her over the rough spot. She watched Luke suspiciously, not sure whether she should trust him.

"Brianna," Luke continued, "no one in Boston calls him Jess. Unless, of course, they're kidding around or madder than hell. Only his friends from law school call him Jess. We call him Mac. He's been Mac since he was a little guy. Mom used to get Jonas and Jess all mixed up—" he paused, as if waiting for her to speak.

She remained silent. Actually she was astounded by Luke's information, yet feeling too weak to respond.

"Yeah," he muttered under his breath. "Guess I ought to wait a while to get into this with you. You need to rest. This is heavy stuff."

"What do you mean?" she whispered.

"Will you answer my question?" he probed. "Did you know him before?"

This time Brianna bobbed her head up and down.

"Where'd you meet him?" Luke asked. As he waited for her to reply, he noticed her blue eyes seemed almost sunken in her white face. He saw the confusion in those eyes, too.

"Brianna," he said gently. "If you knew him before and he didn't recognize you today, I understand this may be difficult for you."

"No. You *don't* understand," she contradicted. Her voice, although weak, held a certain, unmistakable vehemence.

"Yeah. Okay," he allowed, raising his hands in capitulation. "You gonna tell me where you met big brother?"

She inhaled deeply, releasing the breath very slowly. "In Eaton."

"Makes sense," Luke nodded. "Is that where you live?"

"No, I live in Pennsylvania. My aunt and uncle live in Eaton," she explained.

"Do you spend much time there?"

"We vacation there."

"And you met while you were on vacation?"

"Yes," she admitted.

"Yeah," he muttered strangely. "Know him well?"

"It doesn't make any difference how well I knew

him. In case you haven't noticed, he doesn't acknowledge that he knew me. I'm not a fool—''

"No one said you were, Brianna," Luke interrupted firmly. "Besides, there's a very good explanation—''

"Sure," she said, sounding almost sarcastic.

"Yeah. Okay," Luke nodded. "You're hurt because some old friend doesn't recognize you."

Blue sparks flew from her eyes as she impaled Luke with a decidedly angry gaze. It was much more than that. She *was* hurt because he didn't acknowledge her, but she was hurt because he'd disappeared without a word, too. They'd been so close, shared so very much of themselves. . . . She couldn't explain all that to his brother.

"I haven't changed," she said tersely. And that was half true. Physically Brianna Dugan had changed very little in five years. But she'd grown by leaps emotionally. She was no longer naive, carefree, and trusting, as she had once been. She had worked hard to establish her career. Yet those hard-earned differences were not the kind you could see.

"Mac has changed," his brother explained. "And it's not his fault he doesn't know you."

"Doesn't *know* me?" Brianna repeated in disbelief. How could a man be as involved with a woman as Jess had been with her and then not know her five years later?

"Yeah," Luke drawled. "Did you have even the slightest sign he recognized you?"

She was thoughtful. He'd called her blue eyes. He'd quoted Jonson. "At first I thought he did . . ." She shrugged. "But he . . . didn't."

"He can't," Luke informed her.

"*Can't*? Why not?"

"He was in a car accident—"

Brianna fought to suppress a gasp of horror. "When?"

"In August it'll be five years."

"What happened?" Her voice, although faint, sounded urgent.

"A drunk ran a red light, broad-sided Mac's car, plowed into several others. . . ."

She closed her eyes. "The last time I saw him was August—five years ago. . . ."

"He was badly hurt in the accident."

She nodded, listening.

"For days we didn't know if he'd live or die."

Her eyes opened wide. She stared at Luke, the depth of her emotional reaction evident.

"Two of the other people involved in the accident weren't as fortunate," Luke continued as he watched her shudder. "His body healed, Brianna. But his head injuries left him with amnesia—"

"And he doesn't know me." She pronounced each word distinctly, trying to absorb the full meaning.

"It depends on *when* you knew him. He lost about a year. He remembers people from long before. He remembers his friends from law school."

She shook her head back and forth slowly. "But he doesn't remember me, Luke. I only met him . . . in June."

She felt relief rushing through her body. In spite of her persistent weariness, it was almost uplifting, as if someone had finally removed a great burden from her shoulders. After all this time she understood why Jess hadn't kept his promise. He hadn't made a conscious decision to abandon her then or ignore her today. Her emotions swung to an unbelievable high, then, like a pendulum, came sweeping swiftly down as she realized the whole situation.

Jess not only didn't recognize her, he didn't know her. She was a stranger to him. On the heels of elation, an all-encompassing sadness engulfed her.

"You're tired, aren't you?" Luke asked. "Why don't you go back to sleep?"

Brianna nodded again. Her eyelids felt as if they had lead weights on them. She was beyond tired. She was so weak. Sleep would be welcome.

As he rose from the bed, her eyes flew open. "Luke," she said, sounding oddly desperate. "You won't . . . say anything to him, will you?"

"No, Brianna," he assured her. "I won't say anything."

"Thanks," she murmured, closing her eyes once more.

"Brianna, before you fall asleep—" Luke hedged, "you should know he doesn't talk about the accident or about that time in his life. He prefers not to relive the horror. Do you still vacation in Eaton?"

Again she simply nodded her head.

"Mac hasn't gone back in more than four years. He doesn't deal well with his situation. He's always sought logical explanations for everything. This . . . condition is difficult for anyone to explain or understand, especially him. Please remember that."

"I will," she murmured faintly.

Luke stayed with Brianna until she fell asleep again. He was on his way out of the bedroom when his brother came in.

"How's our guest?" Mac asked as he sank into

Sara's plush boudoir chair and stretched his long legs onto the cushion.

"She was awake for a while, but she's really weak, big brother."

"Sara said she had some soup."

"Chicken noodle isn't a magic potion, Mac."

"She's sick, isn't she?"

"Yeah," Luke responded shaking his head. "I think she is."

Mac pursed his lips and blew out a long, loud breath of air.

"I never asked if she was traveling alone or with someone. I assumed she simply needed to eat. . . . Although I recall thinking she looked too pale." His thick eyebrows bunched as he pondered the situation. "Surely there must be someone who would want to know she's here. Has anyone tried to contact her family? Sara's so conscientious I expect she remembered to ask Brianna about that before she left," he said, answering his own question. "Why don't I call her. While I'm on the phone, check Brianna's purse for identification. No sense waking her. She obviously needs the sleep."

"Okay," Luke agreed. "Her handbag is here on the desk."

"I'll call from the other room so I don't disturb her."

Luke had Brianna's wallet opened by the time his brother quietly closed the bedroom door. He found the information he needed without any trouble and moments later was scribbling down the address and phone number printed on her checks.

He didn't like going through Brianna Dugan's handbag. He felt as if he were snooping. When he finished copying her phone number, he intended to return the wallet to its place. Then a picture of a small boy caught his eye and he was temporarily distracted.

He studied the picture curiously, wondering what it was that bothered him. He thought the child looked familiar, but he didn't know why. He flipped through other pictures, still thinking about the little boy.

There was a family photograph of a man, woman, and little girl, one of a baby dressed in blue, and another of Brianna and the woman in the family group. Luke studied the photo of Brianna and the woman, deciding they must be sisters. Both had sable-colored hair, similar facial features, and similar smiles.

And then he flipped back to the picture of the small boy for a second look, examining the face more closely this time. There was something about the child's green eyes. . . .

"Sara didn't realize Brianna was ill. She thought she was dealing with exhaustion. As a matter of fact, Mom apparently asked Brianna if she needed to see a doctor. Brianna declined," Mac reported, startling Luke as he walked back into the room.

Luke had been so engrossed in the picture he hadn't heard a sound. As his eyes met his brother's he realized why the image of the little boy had intrigued him. He flipped the wallet shut and tucked it back inside the handbag.

"I found a phone number. You gonna call?" Luke asked, staring oddly at his elder brother.

"That was the whole idea," Mac responded sarcastically. "What's wrong with you?"

"I guess I'm more tired than I thought."

"Go get some sleep, then. I'll sit with Brianna."

"Why'd you bring her home?" Luke inquired unexpectedly.

Mac shrugged. "I'm not sure. . . . She fainted in my arms. She said she'd missed a meal. I was on my way to dinner. It seemed like a good idea. Mom never objects when a guest joins us at mealtime."

"You could have put her in a cab or, if you were feeling so gallant, escorted her to her hotel."

He dragged his fingers through his thick auburn hair, then nodded thoughtfully. "I could have—"

"But you didn't."

"No," he replied, shaking his head slowly back and forth. "I was already late."

"Bull," Luke charged. "You know how to use the phone. You could have called to say you'd been delayed."

"You're right. I could have . . ." Mac hedged.

"But?"

He rose from the chair and turned away from Luke, moving toward the bed as if he were drawn to her. Again his long fingers raked through his hair. He stared down at Brianna, at her lovely delicate features, at her soft, pale skin, at the silken hair nestled against the pillowcase. He couldn't seem to tear his gaze from her. In his eyes she appeared small and helpless, as though she needed him there, to watch over her and keep her safe.

"I can't explain this," he said in a hushed voice. "I couldn't leave her. I didn't even consider that."

"You just picked her up and brought her along."

"Yes."

"I don't think you ever hauled a stray home before."

Mac sort of grunted, agreeing with his brother. "She's much too well dressed to be a stray. She had reservations at the Sheraton—"

"And yet you—"

"Back off, Luke," Mac told him sharply. "I don't know why I did what I did. But I know I'd do it again, especially knowing what I do now. She's not well. She shouldn't be alone in a hotel room—"

"Yeah," Luke interrupted. "On that we agree. So what'd Chris think when you walked in with the dark-haired beauty?"

"She seemed to take it in stride, though I do believe I saw a trace of green in her gray eyes," he admitted, smiling in amusement. "She was quite a bit more possessive than she normally is, don't you think?"

"That's understandable. You and Chris have been an item for two years," Luke reminded him.

"Inviting a stranger to share dinner with your entire family is not a crime."

"Ah, counselor, but such a beautiful stranger," Luke taunted, sounding decidedly wicked.

Mac stared down at Brianna. "Sleeping Beauty," he murmured, voicing his thoughts out loud.

"You *did* notice."

He nodded. "Yes, Luke. I couldn't help but notice she's lovely." He turned to face his brother. "Ever see such pale blue eyes?"

"You're attracted to her, aren't you?"

"Because I asked if you'd noticed her eyes?"

"No. It's more than that, Mac. Answer my question."

The brothers eyed one another in a silent showdown. Luke had reason to be curious. He watched, waiting for an answer. Mac simply glared.

"Well?" Luke prodded.

"She kissed me," he confessed, so quietly the words might have been imagined instead of spoken.

Now Luke's forehead furrowed. "When?"

"As she was coming to," he revealed. "She wound

her arms around my neck. . . ." He closed his eyes, remembering. She'd smelled like heaven. She'd felt as if she were part of him as her lips pressed against his. The kiss they'd shared had an addictive quality. He'd wanted more. And, he realized, if he had not been vaguely conscious of their surroundings, he would have taken more. Even now the memory of that one kiss aroused him.

"Why?" Luke wondered out loud.

"Why?" Mac made a small noise. "Your guess is as good as mine. We're not going to come up with an answer at this hour. Why don't you go get some sleep?" he suggested, seeing evidence of his brother's weariness. "If you run into Mom, tell her I'm staying tonight. I'll watch over Brianna. She's my responsibility. I'm the one who brought her home."

"She's a person, Mac, not a responsibility."

"I didn't mean that the way it sounded."

"I didn't like the way it sounded. And I'm not sure I approve of the way you're handling this situation, either."

Mac glared at him, confusion knitting his brow.

"Think about it, big brother." Luke's voice was quiet with a hint of a challenge in it. "This lady passes out in your arms. You bring her home—for whatever reason. Then you show almost no concern. You spend the entire evening with Chris while your sisters look after your guest. Now, at nearly one o'clock in the morning, you saunter in here to *assume your responsibility*."

"You've left out a few details."

"Yeah? What? That she kissed you? That you think she's lovely? That she has the most beautiful blue eyes you've ever seen? That you're so attracted to her you can't seem to take your eyes off her for more than a minute?" Luke ticked each of these off on his fingers. "All of which only makes your reaction that much more puzzling."

"And how do you suggest I deal with this situation, Luke?" Mac demanded none too quietly. "Should I have rifled Rachel's dresser drawers for a nightgown for my guest? Should I have helped Brianna out of her clothes and into bed? How the hell do you think Chris would have reacted to that? You were the one who reminded me a few minutes ago that I'm involved in a long-standing relationship, right?"

"Jess?"

Luke shook his head, clearly annoyed because his brother had been careless enough to waken Brianna. "I'm going to bed. If I see Mom, I'll pass your message along."

"Night, Brianna," Luke called softly. "He's here now."

# THREE

Jess MacLaren turned to face the diminutive woman lying in his sister's bed.

"I apologize for waking you." His voice was no longer raised, but gentle as he spoke to her. "Luke was chiding me for deserting you. And rightly so. I insisted you come here. I shouldn't have left you."

"Sara and Rachel were good company. Luke was, too, for that matter."

"Perhaps. But I should have made a point to check on you sooner," he emphasized. "And I never asked if anyone was waiting for you at the Sheraton."

"No. I'm alone."

"Is there anyone who might want to know you're here?"

Brianna nodded. "I should call my sister. She was expecting a phone call earlier. By now she's probably gone beyond worried to frantic."

"Would you like me to make the call, or do you feel

up to it? The phone's right over here. Sara invested in a mile-long cord when she was a teenager.''

"I'll do it myself," Brianna said. "You've done plenty."

He shook his head. "All I did was insist you come along and leave you in my sisters' capable hands."

"I appreciate your concern," she told him. "It's nice to have somebody watching out for me."

He studied her closely as she spoke. Concern began to build, furrowing his forehead. The luxurious sable hair that had attracted him initially appeared limp, not merely tousled from sleep. And there was something not quite right about her eyes.

"You feel lousy, don't you?" he guessed.

Brianna nodded. "Would you mind getting me another blanket? I'm cold," she explained softly.

"No problem, blue eyes," he returned. "Do you suppose a hot cup of tea would help?"

"Tea sounds wonderful."

"Are you hungry? I make a wicked turkey sandwich."

"Thanks, but I don't have much appetite. . . ."

Intent eyes scrutinized her flushed face. "I'll get that extra blanket before I make the tea. Don't go away," he teased, striding toward the door.

When he returned, his arms were full of linens. "I thought you might be warmer if we wrapped you in flannel sheets," he explained.

"It's June," Brianna reminded him.

"You said you were cold."

"I didn't mean to inconvenience you. I only wanted an extra blanket."

"It's right here under this pillow," he indicated, nodding his head at the pillow he plopped onto the bed.

''If you sit up, I'll make sure you're warm and cozy. Flannel first,'' he announced, setting to his task.

She allowed him to plump her pillow and arrange the extra one he'd found in the closet. He pulled off the covers, laid the flannel sheet over her, and draped two blankets—one thermal, one woolen—on top of that. Then he covered the blankets with Sara's gaily flowered down comforter, carefully tucking the sides in close to Brianna.

When his stack of linens was depleted, he passed the phone to her and politely asked if she needed anything else. She was almost afraid to answer, for fear he would bring her something. She felt like a tiny caterpillar inside a giant cocoon, and she was certain she looked like some padded monster from a sci-fi movie.

He finally exited the room again. His promise to return echoed repeatedly through her head. His voice and his familiar words struck a chord of remembrance. She blinked back a sudden rush of tears.

He was not hers anymore. He was not promising to return for another lovers' tryst. He was bringing her a cup of hot tea.

An act of fate had torn them apart. It had altered the course of their lives. But both of them had gone forward in spite of the accident.

She wiped the tears from her face. Jess was alive and well. That was all that mattered. She understood why he'd never kept his promise.

But understanding didn't make the scars disappear. . . .

Brianna struggled to sit up. The weight and bulk of the covers hampered her efforts. When she was finally in a comfortable upright position, she pulled the phone into her lap, then stared down at the ring on her left hand, briefly touching it with the index finger of her right hand. Memories threatened to overwhelm her. She fidgeted momentarily with the slim silver band, and willing the memories back into the far corners of her mind, she punched out her sister's number. The phone rang several times before Laura answered.

"Hi, it's me," Brianna said. "Sorry I'm so late."

"Where were you? I was so worried. When you didn't call by six, I called the hotel. I've left messages every hour on the hour since then."

"I was waylaid by a green-eyed commando," Brianna explained.

"What?" Laura demanded.

"I passed out in busy, bustling Beantown." Brianna made light of the situation, trying to maintain a cheerful pretense because she knew how much her sister worried when she traveled.

"What happened? Are you all right?"

"As a matter of fact, I'm not," Brianna admitted. "I must have something. I'm dizzy and weak. I've been sleeping for hours, and now I have the chills."

"Oh, honey," Laura wailed sympathetically. "That's awful. And you're all alone."

"No, Laura," her sister contradicted. "I said I'd been waylaid—"

"Yes, I heard you. By a green-eyed commando—" She broke off abruptly, paused a few seconds, then asked, "Green-eyed?"

"Hmm," Brianna murmured. "I'll explain in detail when I'm home."

"Brianna." Laura sounded stern.

"It's been one of those days, Sis. Running into *him* was—" she hesitated, then laughed. "If I hadn't been lying in his arms because that's where I ended up when

I passed out, I probably would have swooned from surprise."

"Not you. You're a rock," Laura disagreed. "Did you really wake up in *his* arms? Are we talking about—"

"Hmm," Brianna acknowledged softly. "I was astounded when I looked into his eyes. It was like waking up from this strange dream and looking into Noah's eyes."

"Have you told him about Noah?" Laura asked hesitantly.

"No," Brianna responded quickly. "Oh no."

"Why ever not?"

Brianna took a deep breath and exhaled very slowly. Now she wished she had allowed Jess to make this call. She loved Laura, owed her, in fact. But she was much too weary for lengthy explanations and she knew Laura was too concerned to be put off until later.

"Are you in bed?"

"Of course, silly. It's one in the morning."

"I wanted to make sure you were sitting down."

"Brianna, what's wrong?" Laura demanded urgently.

"He doesn't know me."

"What?" her sister shrieked in her ear. "What do you mean he doesn't know you?"

"Laura, listen. Please listen," Brianna begged. "I'd much rather give you the details when I get home. But the way I'm feeling right this minute, I may not be able to travel as soon as I'd like. And I know you won't wait."

"Brianna," Laura sounded threatening.

"He was in an accident—" The words rushed forth before her sister had time to grow more concerned or exasperated. "I don't know the details, but he has amnesia—"

"Amnesia!" Laura shrieked again. "Amnesia? Are you sure this isn't a convenient line? Or an excuse for running out on you?"

"I'm absolutely certain. If you'd met him, Laura, you'd know he'd never resort to a line. He's as honest as a boy scout."

"Brianna—"

"Besides, it was his brother who told me. Jess apparently doesn't care to talk about the accident or his injury. He almost died—"

"Okay. Okay. Maybe it's the truth. What's this about his brother?"

"Well, I'm . . . staying at his parents' home—"

"What?" Laura's voice was raised again.

"Laura, please. You were worried that I was alone. I'm not. There's a house full of very nice people taking turns looking after me. Please don't worry. I promise I'll call tomorrow to keep you posted on my health. Okay?"

"Okay," she agreed reluctantly. "His family is caring for you, Brianna?"

"Hmm," Brianna murmured, nodding in spite of the fact her sister couldn't see her. "How's Noah?"

"He's fine. He and Jenna created this monster pit in the sandbox today. I was afraid if they dug any deeper one of them would be buried alive. Noah said they were excavating for a new road. Imagine that, excavating!" Laura emphasized. "Not exactly little-boy vocabulary."

Brianna smiled to herself. "Noah vocabulary, though. Give him a big hug and kiss for me and tell him we'll go to the beach just as soon as I make the arrangements."

"Are you really, truly all right there?"

"Yes, Laura. These people are doing a superb job

of mothering. They haven't left me alone for a minute until now. Jess is off making tea for me. Don't worry!''

"And you'll call tomorrow?''

"I promise I will," Brianna said solemnly.

Catching sight of a movement out of the corner of her eye, she bid her sister a hasty farewell.

Jess had entered the room carrying a tray laden with a teapot and cups. She swallowed hard, her eyes fastened on him as he approached. He'd changed out of the jacket and slacks he'd worn earlier and was dressed quite casually in a forest green sweat suit that accentuated his unique coloring. Now he looked even more like the man she remembered.

He placed the tray on the desk and lifted the pot to pour the tea. "You reached your sister?''

"Hmm," she acknowledged.

"Everything okay there?''

"Everything's fine at home," she answered truthfully. *The problem is here*, she added to herself.

"I didn't mean to intrude. You were speaking so softly I didn't realize you weren't finished until I was in the room. Your tea is ready.''

"You didn't intrude. I was finished, except for trying to reassure her one last time that I was well taken care of. . . .''

When he handed the cup to Brianna, her fingers brushed the warmth of his large hand. She felt an immediate flush sweep from head to toe as her body responded involuntarily. It was the only bit of warmth running through her. In an effort to distract herself from thinking about his unintentional, but incendiary touch, she took a hasty sip of tea.

He didn't miss a thing. He watched her, focusing on

her shaky hands, the frantic sip of tea, the nervous way her tongue darted out to lick the moisture from her lips.

"This is good," she said. "Honey and lemon?"

"I didn't know what you liked. It's another of Mom's cures."

"And best of all, it's hot," she said, sounding cheerful.

He continued watching her critically as she eased herself carefully back onto the pillows and shut her eyes. He realized the bright lilt in her voice was in direct contrast to her weary appearance.

"What's wrong?"

"I can't seem to get warm. Even the tea and the extra blankets don't seem to be helping."

His immediate response, although Brianna didn't see it, was to strip off the borrowed sweatshirt he wore.

"Lean forward," he commanded gently, reaching to take the teacup from her hands. "Slip this on and we'll see if it helps."

Brianna tugged on the heavy fabric, pulling it down to her hips and wiggling until she was sitting on some of it. Every movement made her shiver more.

"Perfect fit," she announced, turning the sleeves up to uncover her hands.

He chuckled. "Okay, so it's kind of oversized for you. It's the best I can do right now. Sara didn't leave any clothes behind when she moved out. And I don't want to go tiptoeing into Rachel's room and scare her half to death. Believe me, when Rachel yells, she's capable of awakening the entire household, as well as part of the neighborhood."

Brianna laughed with him, watching the merriment fairly dance across his handsome face.

"Thanks," she murmured. "Will you be warm

enough without your shirt?'' Her eyes strayed to the mat of dense auburn hair on his chest. She'd always believed merely looking at him could warm her inside and out. Too bad that wasn't the case tonight.

"No problem. If I get cold, I'll just march up to the tower room and borrow another from Luke. Nothing wakes him once he's asleep. That shirt's his anyway. Besides I was considering wrapping you in my arms until you stopped shivering,'' he admitted.

Her eyebrows raised in surprise. He would have done that five years ago without thinking. But now? Tonight? As much as she wanted to be enfolded in his strong arms, she wasn't sure she should allow it. Another chill swept through her and she shuddered violently.

"Move over,'' he said, suddenly taking the decision out of her hands. "It's worth a try.''

He climbed in bed next to her, pulled her securely against his warm body, and carefully replaced the layers of covers. "Comfortable?'' he inquired, sounding genuinely concerned.

She was pressed so tightly to him that she felt the deep rumble inside his chest as he spoke.

"I am,'' she assured him.

"Warmer?''

*Warmer*? she mused, certain his body heat could roast them both under normal circumstances. "Not yet.''

"We'll give it a while. See if there's anything to that theory about sharing body heat.''

"Do you think it works if the person who's cold is shivering because she's sick?''

"We'll find out, won't we, blue eyes?'' he said, touching one long finger to the side of her face. "Your skin's not cold. As a matter of fact, it feels a tad too warm.''

She rolled her head back against him. "I think I have a fever.''

"I wouldn't be surprised.''

"My lucky day,'' she quipped. She felt, more than heard, his chuckle.

"What brought you to Boston?''

"I've agreed to make an appearance and sign autographs at a bookstore here.''

"You are in no condition to do any such thing!''

"Hmm,'' she agreed. "I realize that.''

"You're still shivering,'' he said, feeling the chills rack her body again.

Brianna rubbed her hands up and down on her arms trying to chase the chills away. Nothing worked. After another violent shudder, he gathered her closer and tucked the blankets in tighter.

"You didn't realize you were getting sick this afternoon while you were shopping, did you?''

"I thought I was just hungry.''

"Why didn't you eat?''

Brianna smiled. "You'll probably think this is stupid, but I hate to fly. It's one of those dreaded phobias we all have but hate to admit. Anyway, I get so crazy before I fly that if I dared to eat, I'd probably make myself sick. So I didn't eat. Then my flight was delayed . . . and I didn't get to Logan until just before noon. There was so much I wanted to see in Boston— This is my first trip—'' She shrugged.

"I'll be glad to show you some of the sights. I'm a native. Born and raised—'' he broke off suddenly, oddly.

She wasn't sure why he'd stopped.

"Thanks, but no thanks," she said. "I don't date men with previous commitments."

She felt the movement of the pillow behind them and guessed he was running his fingers through his thick hair in frustration.

"Your decision, Brianna. I'll respect it. However, I see it differently, not as a date."

She shook her head slightly and he continued speaking.

"I don't believe my relationship with Chris creates a problem. And before you get your dander up, you should know I'm not committed to her in any formal way. We've been dating exclusively. People assume we've made a commitment, but we haven't. In any case, that's neither here nor there. I'm offering to show you Boston through the eyes of a native."

"No, thank you, Mac," she replied, calling upon her innermost reserves. She wanted nothing more than to tour Boston at his side. She wanted to spend time alone with him, to sit and chat with him as she was now. But that wasn't possible.

"If I were Chris," she explained, "I certainly wouldn't want you escorting someone else."

"Possessive, huh?" he teased. "Brianna, I have a good relationship with Chris, but I'm not bound to her. And I deal with female clients all the time. Chris is secure enough not to feel threatened."

"I'm not a threat. I've said no," she replied tersely.

"Don't you have any *friends* who are men?"

"No. I don't," she stated quietly, trying to rein in her turbulent emotions. "I live in small-town America."

"As in post office boxes and church suppers?"

"Exactly," she acknowledged. "As a matter of fact, I missed a church supper tonight."

Again Brianna felt his low chuckle more than heard it.

"Where is this storybook town?" he asked, a hint of laughter in his deep voice.

"In the mountains of Pennsylvania," she answered. "It's a little town, like others in the mountains, whose lumber mills are its sole support. It's quaint, almost like living in a time warp. The pace is slow. Most of the folks have never been close to a city the size of Boston, and they don't even care," she finished, suppressing a yawn.

"I don't need a more definite hint than that," he said. "Time for lights out. You need your rest."

"I am tired," she admitted. "Even though I'm sure I slept most of the evening."

"Sara said you looked exhausted and she probably shouldn't have kept talking with you."

"At least I didn't embarrass myself and fall asleep in front of her."

"You mean Rachel *talked* you to sleep?" he asked, laughing outright.

Brianna nodded.

"If I'm not careful, I will, too. Okay. No more conversation. Close your beautiful eyes. I'll get the light."

Brianna didn't close her eyes. She watched as he left the bed and strode into the alcove to reach the lamp switch. Her eyes feasted on him. On his muscled arms and broad back, which were completely exposed, on his long legs clad in a loose-fitting pair of sweats . . .

And then the lights went out. The room was engulfed in darkness.

She heard the quiet thud of his feet on the carpet. The mattress sagged as he crawled back into the small double bed.

"You're still shivering," he whispered as he drew her up against his warm body.

"Only a little now."

"Snuggle closer," he suggested. "Wrap your arms around me and lie across my chest."

It was an easy thing to do. She'd done it before, but tonight she hesitated.

"It's okay," he assured her, gathering her so tightly to him she almost gasped at the intimacy of the gesture.

She tensed involuntarily. Time had passed. Their lives had changed. He was involved with another woman.

"Relax," he commanded softly. "Go to sleep. I'll keep you warm."

He felt her body gradually relaxing against his own as she drifted off to sleep. And he realized he liked the way she felt in his arms.

She was small and slender, like a fragile doll. At the moment she was lying so securely against his naked chest that he could not help noticing her size or her physical attributes. He was very much aware of her femininity. In spite of her delicate structure, she was curvaceous. Where his hand rested on her tiny waist, he could feel the gentle flare of her hips. And he couldn't ignore the undeniable swell of her breasts where they molded against the wall of his chest.

Although the woman was lovely in every respect, her eyes were her most arresting feature. From the first moment she'd looked at him, he'd been captivated by her pale eyes. He was repeatedly drawn to them. And he realized each time he ventured a gaze, he fell into their silent depths.

*Free-falling,* he mused. *That's what looking into Brianna Dugan's eyes is like. Free-falling.*

As he pictured her face in the darkness, he felt his stomach clench with a peculiar anxiety. The sensation was not totally foreign to him, but it was uncommon.

She made him feel protective, as he did toward Sara and Rachel, yet different. More intense. He didn't understand this feeling and that bothered him. He liked to have control of his feelings, and his destiny, as well. He'd learned that wasn't always possible; still, he preferred to be the one calling the shots.

Bringing home this beautiful bundle had not been in his plans. Yet here she was, lying in his arms. He wanted an explanation for her presence just as much as Luke had. But he had none.

He seemed to be acting without a plan. That wasn't like him. It made him feel out of control. The only other time in his life he'd felt this way, the Fates had dealt him a lousy hand. He'd played it out and gone forward, choosing not to dwell on something he needed to forget.

He had no explanation for his actions now, except some feeble excuse that he'd acted on instinct. Acted . . . or reacted? She'd definitely drawn a reaction from him. He was concerned about her. She obviously wasn't feeling well. But why was he holding her now? He'd acted instinctively, involuntarily. And holding her close seemed the natural thing to do. But why?

Was it because she was cold? Or was it because the touch of her lips enchanted him? Or did he simply need an excuse to hold her this close to his heart?

He realized then she held him, too. Physically she clung to him, her slender fingers curled around his neck. Her touch was light, yet possessive. But she held him emotionally as well—gripped him with a powerful emotional response.

He couldn't leave her. He was involved. He had to stay.

Not that he should. Chris was the one he should be holding.

He shifted his weight on the bed, inhaling the sweet fragrance of Brianna's hair. She still smelled like heaven. . . .

He couldn't seem to divorce himself from the allure of the delicate beauty even though he knew holding her was wrong. He knew there was no way he could ever explain his actions to Chris. How could he begin to tell her he was strangely drawn to another woman? Inexplicably drawn, with the force of a need as elemental as breathing.

There were few things in his life he felt this strongly about. His family, of course, evoked powerful feelings. His home and family were an integral part of the person he had grown to be. Nothing was more important to Jess MacLaren than his family. Nothing measured up to the feelings he had for his parents, his brothers, his sisters. Nothing.

He knew that. He'd accepted it years earlier. But now, as he pondered his present dilemma, he realized how significant that fact was.

His feelings for Chris didn't hold him as tightly as his love of family. In the stillness of the night, he admitted to himself there were weaknesses in his relationship with Chris.

Unbidden, a restlessness began to grow. He didn't understand the feeling, but he recognized it. He'd felt it before on occasion. It wasn't a feeling he could ever hope to explain to anyone, but it existed. It came from deep inside and weighed upon him, sometimes so heavily he thought he could not carry the burden of frustration.

Tonight was not so bad. The feeling was there, close to the surface, yet more understated than it usually was. And holding Brianna in his arms seemed to ease the tension.

He rested his chin in her sweet-smelling hair, then drew in a long breath of air.

Holding her felt right. And he was too tired to care if it wasn't.

# FOUR

He turned the big glass knob slowly and eased the door open, careful to make as little noise as possible. He was so intent on shutting the door behind himself that he didn't notice her at first. But when he did, he froze on the spot.

She was beautiful.

Never before had he felt his breath catch the way it did when he stepped into his sister's room and saw Brianna. She was standing in front of Sara's doll collection brushing her long sable hair. His eyes followed the downward sweep of the brush as it moved through her silken tresses. She looked like a life-size doll crowned with rich dark hair. Her alabaster skin and sparkling eyes added to the illusion. And the nightgown she'd borrowed from Rachel completed the picture. It was a prim, high-necked flannel with a row of tiny buttons all the way down the front and eyelet edging the collar and cuffs. The fabric was a pleasing shade of light blue, close to the color of Brianna's eyes. But nothing could match the delightful sparkle he found in those eyes when his gaze met with hers.

"Good morning, Sleeping Beauty," he said. "Feeling better or are you going to swoon at my feet?"

"If you promise to catch me again, I'll swoon," she dared to tease.

Jess MacLaren's eyebrows rose considerably. He had not expected this demure-looking woman to return his verbal sparring so boldly. As he watched, her bright smile faded and he witnessed a marked change in her demeanor. Confusion clouded her eyes. Her posture became rigid. "Are you all right?"

"I'm feeling much better, thank you." It was the truth. Physically she was feeling better, but she'd just experienced an emotional decline. She had responded to Jess, not Mac, the proper Boston lawyer. His reaction reminded her that things were different. While she wanted nothing more than to step forward, waltz into his arms, and be enfolded by his warmth, his strength, his passion, the man who stood before her, looking so very concerned, had changed. He was not her lover.

"I didn't expect to find you up and about this morning. Are you hungry?" he inquired, studying her carefully, as if he did not believe she truly was feeling better.

"Hmm." She nodded, struggling to find the polite mask she wore for strangers. Right now she felt a desperate need to hide behind it so Jess wouldn't see the sadness washing through her.

"I'll bring you breakfast," he offered. "But I want you to get back in bed. Take it easy, in case you haven't fully recovered."

"I said I was feeling better," she insisted.

"No argument. Back to bed. I don't want you taking chances."

For some reason, perhaps because she was feeling exposed, Brianna bristled at his tone. "I am an adult, Mr. MacLaren. And I'm perfectly capable of taking care of myself. . . ."

"It's Mac," he reminded her. "And your perfect capabilities failed you yesterday."

Brianna ran the brush through her hair, avoiding his eyes. She knew she shouldn't be annoyed. None of this was his fault. He'd come to her rescue, he'd stayed with her, held her when she was cold.

"I'm sorry," she said, slowly raising her eyes to meet with his again. "I didn't mean to sound ungrateful."

Something about her struck a chord within him. He knew he was attracted to this woman. Not just by her beauty and not just by her bewitching blue eyes or her gentle voice either. The entire woman, the essence of her, cried out to something deep within him—and he responded.

"I believe you could convince me to forgive you a thousand times," he declared quietly.

Brianna's chin came up and her eyes widened in surprise.

"Perhaps a thousand and one," he said, grinning.

She studied him. Took in everything, from the up-turned corners of his mouth to the light dancing in his malachite eyes. It was all familiar.

Maybe Jess wasn't so far away.

"I'll bring you breakfast?" He actually asked permission.

"Thanks." She nodded just once, then watched as he walked out of the room and closed the door.

"Oh, Jess," she murmured. "I love you far too much."

No sooner were the words spoken than reality hit her full force.

She had been in bed with him last night. It had not been the burning physical experience of her youth, but she had been snuggling, comfortably, in the shelter of his strong arms.

She ought to be embarrassed. And yet, she wasn't. After all, she'd slept in his arms before. She had, in fact, been intimate with him a number of times. She could not be embarrassed about lying innocently in his arms.

But she wasn't ready to repeat the past. And he had promised to return. . . .

She tucked the hairbrush into her purse, hastily dabbed makeup on her already scrubbed face, and grabbed the rich velour robe she'd found on the bathroom door this morning. Then she slipped quietly out of Sara's room to search for the kitchen.

It wasn't hard to find. The smell of bread toasting and coffee perking lured her in the right direction.

When she entered the room, he was pouring the steaming brown liquid from an oversized pot on the long counter. He wheeled to face her as if he sensed her presence.

"What's wrong?"

She couldn't explain that she hadn't dared to be alone with him in the bedroom. "I'm fine," she assured him, hugging her arms around herself. "I thought it would be simpler if I ate in the kitchen."

"Good morning, Brianna." Libby MacLaren turned to greet her. "I'm glad you're feeling better. Mac has a tray ready for you. Please don't hesitate to ask if you need anything else. With the crowd I feed it's necessary to keep my larder stocked.''

Brianna smiled graciously at the older woman, then glanced toward the tray sitting on the massive kitchen table. It was loaded with food. "Thank you. I don't think I'm quite as hungry as that."

"Mac fixed the tray. It's suited to his gigantic appetite. Don't feel as if you have to finish it.''

"I couldn't, even if I tried," Brianna confessed, laughing softly.

"Would you like to eat in front of the fire?" he asked. "There's a gas fireplace in the den. It only takes a minute to light. We'll go in there?''

She nodded her consent. "Sounds cozy.''

"Warm, too. This old house is a bit chilly until the sun's up higher. Will you join us, Mom?" he asked.

"You two go ahead. I shared an early breakfast with your dad and Ethan before they left.''

As he lit the fire, Brianna settled comfortably in a corner of the love seat. Her eyes slid, inch by inch, from his face, down over the Boston Celtics T-shirt covering his broad chest, on toward his sweatpants, then dropped to his bare feet.

When she'd had her fill of him, she realized he was watching her, too. She felt herself blush in embarrassment and quickly averted her eyes.

Nodding toward the breakfast tray, she asked, "What are you feeding me?''

Thick auburn eyebrows rose suggestively. "Are you too weak to feed yourself?''

She knew she deserved that. Hadn't she teased him when they were alone in the bedroom?

Her eyes locked with his, acknowledging the heightened tension flowing between them. His look said he felt it too.

In addition to dealing with that knowing look, her body was doing things it hadn't done in years. She'd done more harm than good with her thorough inspection of his anatomy. But she'd been compelled to study him, drawn to his form even though she'd seen him nearly naked dozens of times, even though she'd practically memorized every magnificent inch of his body five years earlier.

Time had passed. Their relationship was no longer intimate. In her mind she knew that, but her body responded to his presence. Deep inside the longing had begun, and even now was growing, spiraling steadily.

His gaze was unwavering. She knew she had to halt the mounting flow of tension, so she attempted to tactfully steer the subject away from their bodies.

"Your house is beautiful." Her eyes shifted to the old woodwork around the tall windows and deep window seats.

"This is my parents' home," he reminded her. "I live in Beacon Hill." Deep grooves appeared in his forehead suddenly. "Didn't you tell me this is your first trip to Boston?"

"Yes," she acknowledged. "But I've heard about Beacon Hill. And I like to familiarize myself with a place before I visit."

"Then I won't bore you with details," he told her. "My town house is perfect for me now, but I'd like to have a place like this when I'm married and have a half dozen kids of my own."

"A half dozen?" She nearly choked.

"I like kids. And family is important to me," he explained.

She couldn't resist his warm smile or the twinkle in his spectacular eyes. She returned his smile easily enough. But his comment about family and kids of his own hit too close to home, forcing her to look the other way as quickly as possible.

"You'd better eat before it gets cold," he instructed, using the same tone a parent uses when coaxing a child to eat.

Brianna continued smiling as she fixed a plate of food. Jess would always be like that. He simply expected other people to follow his advice. He didn't mean to be overbearing, and in most cases he wasn't.

She nibbled obediently at an oatmeal muffin, not at all surprised to discover it was delicious. She'd expected as much from Libby MacLaren.

He watched until he was satisfied she was going to eat, not merely go through the motions to appease him. When she took a larger bite, he helped himself to a thick slice of bacon, then finished his orange juice in two big gulps.

"I woke just before dawn roasting beneath that mountain of covers." He leaned back, extended his long legs, and crossed them at the ankle. "The heat was unbearable. You were restless, but your skin didn't feel hot anymore, so I pulled the comforter off. I wasn't comfortable leaving you alone. . . ." He paused momentarily, shrugging off the feeling that washed through him as he tried to explain his actions. It was the same strong, protective feeling that had gripped him during the night.

"I stretched out in Sara's boudoir chair for a while, until I admitted to myself I wouldn't be able to go back to sleep. By then you were sleeping peacefully. So I came in here and searched the library shelves for your book." He paused again, watching Brianna for reaction.

"I assume from the look in your eyes that your search was successful?" She stabbed at a piece of grapefruit and caught a glimpse of him raking his fingers through his hair. The gesture was the one outward indication of inner turmoil that escaped his remarkable control.

"Yes, it was. I started reading because I was curious after hearing Sara and Rachel heap praise on you last evening. I wondered what you wrote about." He looked at her then as if he expected a response.

She swallowed, glancing down at the food in front of her.

"Life," she said softly. "The tricks fate deals us and how we choose to live with them." Her chin came up and she faced him, thankful he couldn't read her mind. Her book was her own story, but she didn't dare elaborate or supply him with a more accurate explanation.

"Have the Fates been so unkind to you, Brianna?"

"Yes and no. I've learned to live with the Fates, to accept what is and what will be."

For a moment her statement hung between them in silence.

"I suppose I have, too," he admitted. "It doesn't do any good to dwell on a past we can't change. . . . I should know. I've had a little run-in with the Fates myself. Perhaps that's why I became so engrossed in the story."

"Did you?"

He gave a slight nod of his head. "I was hooked on page one. I don't like loose ends. I wanted to know more."

Brianna smiled, pleased he'd responded that way, yet apprehensive as well.

"Do you have a child?" he asked, feeling reluctant about probing into her personal life, but compelled to ask nonetheless.

"I have a son." Her soft voice resounded in the quiet room. The hissing of the fire was the only other noise.

He studied her closely, puzzling over what it was that intrigued him so much and wondering why his gut tightened when she spoke. He knew it wasn't merely the sound of her voice this time. He thought it might be a reaction to her revelation.

"That explains it," he finally said.

"What?"

"I wondered how you wrote so convincingly from a mother's point of view."

"I suppose it comes naturally," she allowed.

He glanced at her left hand for the first time, surprised to see she wore a diamond ring. He hadn't noticed it yesterday. Of course, yesterday he hadn't been able to get past her eyes.

"You're . . . married?"

"No, I'm not."

"Divorced?"

As a knot of tension twisted inside her, Brianna shook her head.

"Engaged?" His gentle tone was tinged with curiosity.

She shook her head again.

"That's not an engagement ring?" he queried, puzzled.

"Well, yes, it is," she hedged, looking down at her plate momentarily. Then she lifted her gaze to meet his directly. "He left me. . . . But he never actually broke the engagement."

"And you didn't return the ring?"

"I—" she began. "No."

"So that exquisite diamond is just for show? To keep the hungry wolves at bay?"

"No," she denied. "That's not why I wear it."

He rubbed his hand across his chin, sensing a change in her demeanor, as if she'd retreated behind an invisible wall. He realized he didn't like distance. He wanted to get closer, wanted to know more about her. So he continued.

"Is your estranged fiancé the father of your child?" As he watched, she swallowed hard. Her chin tilted upward slightly.

"Yes."

One word. Had she said only one word? Somehow that softly spoken word exploded in the quiet of the room. Its impact echoed inside his head. She had answered him, but he needed more. "Where is he? Do you see him? Does he see his son?"

"He doesn't know he has a son."

She responded to his rapid volley of questions before he even realized he'd spoken out loud. He was amazed she remained so calm. His insides were churning. Had he heard her correctly? Had she said "He doesn't know"?

"How could you neglect to tell a man something as important as that?" he demanded, glaring at her, unable to disguise his disapproval.

"Fate never gave me the opportunity to tell him," she said, her soft voice even, regulated.

Although her surface poise appeared unruffled, the pale eyes watching him had clouded over as if she had withdrawn further behind the invisible wall. Almost as if she were hiding something. He had a strong urge to tear down the barrier, to see behind it.

And he was angry that she'd constructed a buffer between them. He preferred the closeness he'd felt last night or the passion he'd experienced when she'd kissed him. He knew his emotions were ever so slowly undermining his control, but short of leaving the room, he saw no way to restore his normal composure.

He had to learn more about this woman. He had to question her to understand why she had done something as incomprehensible as keeping her child to herself.

"Where is he?" he demanded.

"My son?" she asked, seeming disconcerted for the first time.

"Yes, your son." He forced out the words, feeling barely civil.

"He's with Laura."

"Who's Laura?" He felt his patience taking wing, too.

"My sister," she replied, her tone defensive.

"Don't you take care of your own child?"

"Yes, I take care of him, but he doesn't travel with me," she tried to explain.

"Why not? You're his mother," he snapped. Now he knew he was near the edge. Tension pulsed through him as if it had a life of its own.

"I don't think he should—" she began.

"What a life for a kid!" he scoffed, cutting her off. "No father. And a part-time mother who looks like a kid herself!" His anger had taken control. There was no way he could keep the condemnation out of his voice.

He saw a hint of turbulence, a few blue sparks flashing in Brianna's eyes, before her temper rose to the surface. It was but a fleeting warning. All at once she flew at him like a shot, stopping only inches in front of him. She was like a small tornado facing him, screaming in anger, "How dare you insult me like that, Jess! You weren't there. I had no control over my situation. Laura and Tom gave us a home. I'm there with him most of the time. And when I can't be, I know he gets the love and care and security he needs from them."

He was astounded by her unexpected flare-up. He knew he'd pushed. He couldn't help himself. And for the most part she'd remained self-possessed and remote.

Now she stood, not beautifully serene, but rigid, glaring at him in righteous fury while he stared back at her in amazement. He was almost certain he hadn't heard one single word of her tirade.

Suddenly she pivoted and stormed out of the room.

He let her go without a word. It was one of the few times in his life he'd found himself speechless. He knew he was responsible for arousing her ire, but he made no move to detain her.

He retrieved his coffee from the lamp table, sipping but not really tasting, staring blankly at the doorway. Then realizing he held the mug in his hand, he peered into it, as if it would supply him with answers.

When Luke joined him, he still had not moved.

"Mom said you and Brianna were having breakfast in here. Where is she?"

"Hmm?"

"Where'd you hide Brianna? Mom said she was in here with you."

He shrugged one shoulder slightly.

"That is not an answer."

"What?" His voice reflected the confusion he felt.

"Yeah," Luke muttered under his breath. "What happened to our guest?" he asked, repeating each word distinctly.

This time Mac responded. "She got mad and left."

"Why don't you tell me what happened," Luke suggested, sensing something wasn't right. His brother spoke too quietly, as if he were still distracted.

"I insulted her."

Luke studied his sibling thoughtfully. In most situations, he maintained total control and a near-perfect calm. Luke had always envied that attribute. Now, however, Mac appeared unnaturally tense and edgy. He'd seen him this way very few times in their adult lives.

"Do you want to explain this?" he asked. "You brought a very attractive woman home to dinner. Now you're telling me you insulted her. Not exactly proper guest relations, big brother. How did you manage to be so gauche?"

Mac shook his head slowly side to side. "I implied I thought she was a lousy mother," he confessed.

"Just how well do you know her?"

"I explained yesterday." He raised his eyes, impaling his brother with a hard look. "She passed out downtown. I thought she needed to eat. I brought her home. Why the hell do you keep harping on that? I don't know her any better than you do."

"But—"

"But what, Luke?"

"You pass judgment on her? You think you're capable of assessing whether or not she's a *good* mother? How could you possibly know?" he demanded.

"I couldn't."

"It bothers you, doesn't it?"

"I suppose it does."

"Why?" Luke queried, still watching him closely.

Mac sucked in a large breath, filling his lungs gradually, as if he were stalling for time. He appeared to consider the matter at great length before he answered. "I have no idea why. I wish I did."

"I think it's attraction."

He pursed his lips and stared absently at Luke. "Perhaps you're right. Perhaps it is attraction. But I'd be a fool to act on it. I wouldn't want to hurt Chris."

"Yeah," Luke agreed, nodding his head.

"I suppose I owe Brianna one hell of an apology."

"Indeed you do, big brother," he agreed. "Indeed you do."

"Don't rub it in," he muttered half under his breath. "I'll go talk to her right now."

"Don't push," Luke advised.

"What?"

"No steamroller tactics."

"I won't push. I'll apologize for my temper."

"Yeah, good place to start," Luke agreed.

"Don't push." Mac grinned as he rose to his feet.

Normally Brianna took things in stride, accepted what was dealt her, and coped with it as best she could. She almost never raised her voice. It simply was not natural for her to be as angry as she had been with Jess. But this situation brought all her emotions, old, buried ones as well as fresh, new ones, to the surface. Who could blame her for shouting at him when he'd revealed his disgust at the way he *thought* she was raising her child?

She had done the best she could for Noah. She was

proud of the success she'd achieved with her writing and what it meant in terms of a future for the two of them. Of course, Brianna couldn't blurt out an explanation to Jess, not without revealing his part in the drama of their lives and not without hurting him. She knew she could never intentionally do anything to cause Jess MacLaren more pain. He'd had enough.

She'd barely finished rationalizing her behavior when a sharp knock on the door startled her. Before she could cross the room, Jess's tall frame filled her vision. His appearance was unexpected considering their stormy parting.

"May I come in?" he inquired, a large measure of reserve evident in his deep voice. Reserve itself was an anomaly.

"You already have."

He paused on the threshold, simply staring. She stood in front of Sara's doll collection, as she had earlier. Again it struck him how much she looked as if she belonged there. She appeared fragile and vulnerable, and if her eyes had not been filled with so much emotion, he could have mistaken her for a life-size doll.

He recognized the tug of sensual awareness at once. Although he wanted to deny its existence, he couldn't. It was too strong. The smile he had fixed in place before he knocked disappeared.

"I came to apologize," he explained. "I had no business judging your competence as a parent. No one knows anyone well enough for that. I tend to make hasty judgments sometimes, on a personal level, expecting others to share my principles. It's something I would never consider professionally." He turned his palms up and shrugged his broad shoulders, then stepped closer to her. "Will you accept my apology?"

She didn't respond immediately. Instead she studied his beloved face with a prolonged, silent scrutiny. Here was a man who had known her well enough five years earlier to give her not only his avowed love, but also a child. Now he didn't know her well enough to judge whether she was a good mother to that child.

*We're the same people, only older*, she thought. *I love him more now than I ever thought possible and he doesn't remember loving me. . . .*

"Brianna?"

His low-timbred voice startled her, rousing her from her abstraction. She focused unhurriedly and found his magnetic gaze fastened on her. The look in his eyes touched her.

"I'll accept your apology," she told him softly.

"Good. I'm sorry I upset you. I'm usually more tolerant of nontraditional lifestyles," he explained. "Are you still upset by my opinionated remarks?"

"No," she answered without much conviction. His intense scrutiny disturbed her. "No," she repeated, taking a deep breath before she could trust herself to speak.

"I . . . guess I owe you an apology for losing my temper. That isn't at all like me," she explained. "I'm . . . very defensive when it comes to my son."

"I understand," he said. "Maternal instinct?"

"Exactly," she murmured, her eyes locked with his as unspoken understanding passed between them. In spite of their silent exchange, she wrestled with emotions spiraling ever deeper.

He was the first to speak again. "Now that you're feeling better, have you made plans?"

She nodded. "I think I'm going to lounge around

today. Go back to my hotel. Not exert myself at all. And if I'm feeling better in the morning, I'll go home."

"There's no reason to stay in a strange hotel room when you're more than welcome here."

"My luggage—" Brianna began.

"We'll see that you get it," he informed her. "And at the risk of sounding improper again, will you allow me to give you a ride to the airport when you leave? You are flying, aren't you?"

"Yes, I am," she assured him. "Thanks for the offer. I'd appreciate a ride."

"I'm glad to know you're willing to compromise."

"I hadn't realized I was."

"You'll have to be seen in public with me," he teased. As soon as he said the words, regret engulfed him. He didn't know if he suddenly regretted his relationship with Chris or if he felt guilty throwing it at Brianna. Whichever, he fervently wished he could recall the words, even though they'd been said in jest.

She coped quite well with his thoughtless remark. She'd been staring at him rather blatantly and noticed the grimace of remorse that followed his casual taunt. She knew Jess was not an unfeeling cad, even if he'd sounded like one. His remark hurt because it was not only a reminder of his relationship with another woman, but also a reminder of what she'd lost. She realized he hadn't intended to wound her. After all, he had no way of knowing the depths of her feelings.

"I can handle it," she returned, meeting his gaze head-on.

"I'm certain you can," he said. "I believe in spite of your porcelain doll appearance, you're probably a gutsy lady. As I read your book, I understood why my mother and sisters were so impressed." He paused, searching her face. "You lay all your feelings out in print, don't you?"

Brianna only nodded. Her eyes never left his.

"Does the story—" he broke off awkwardly. "Does it parallel your own story?"

"Largely," she replied, looking away uncomfortably.

"You had your baby by yourself?"

"My sister was with me."

"But the father was absent."

"If I'm not mistaken, didn't we argue this point earlier?" She stole a fleeting glance in his direction.

"I was rude, Brianna," he confessed. "And I apologized."

"And you brought it up again."

"I suppose I'm still curious. A beautiful, intelligent woman, with a child, fending for herself?"

"Not exactly, I live with my sister and her husband."

"Don't you ever wonder what it would be like if you had told him?"

Brianna eyed him thoughtfully. Although she was disconcerted by the turn of the conversation, his voice sounded caring, concerned, and tactful at the same time.

"The choice was taken from me," she stated calmly. "But, to answer your question, yes. When I watch my son with his uncle, I wonder how he'd interact with his father."

She thought for a moment he wasn't listening. He seemed to be staring blindly at the dolls on Sara's shelves. Then she realized he had indeed heard her but was deep in thought.

"The dedication in your book, *To Noah—the man who holds my hand on this lonely road—with love.*

Who's Noah? Your brother-in-law? You dedicated your book to him, so I assume he's someone special.''

Her voice was quiet and steady as she answered. ''Noah is the most important person in my life. He's the reason I wrote the book, the reason I make it through each crisis I face. Noah's love makes it possible for me to live each day. As long as we're together, I'm not alone.'' She paused to stare intently at Jess's beloved face. ''Noah is my son.''

She wanted desperately to continue, to tell him Noah was his son, too, but she knew that wasn't fair. He wasn't looking back.

''Does your entire world revolve around your son?''

''Mostly,'' she answered truthfully. ''But I'm here, aren't I?''

He stared at her as if he were trying to unravel a mystery. In fact, he felt like he was. He was curious about the woman, the mother, the author. He felt compelled to learn more.

''It seems to me, Brianna,'' he began, ''you're here simply because you've written a very moving account of a woman's love for her child. Sure, you detail the hardships of being a young, single mother. But the dominant theme, as far as I've read, is the mother's total devotion to her child. Am I wrong, or is that the real Brianna Dugan?''

''It's very close,'' she admitted, her voice little more than a whisper. ''But I'm not a one-dimensional person—''

''I didn't say you were,'' he interrupted. ''Nor did I mean to imply that. Your heroine isn't one-dimensional either. I suspect behind those lovely eyes lies a woman with great depth. Although I doubt seriously I could prove that this morning," he added. "You look very tired."

"I am tired. It must be directly related to whatever it was that knocked me for a loop yesterday."

"Why don't you rest?" he suggested. "I'll go clean up our breakfast dishes."

"You don't strike me as the domestic type," she observed, remembering the apartment he'd kept in Eaton. It had been clean but cluttered.

"I'm not. But a mother shouldn't have to pick up after her grown son."

She watched him through caring eyes. He was so near and yet so far away.

"Perhaps I ought to get some sleep," she commented as he ambled toward the door.

"Sweet dreams, Sleeping Beauty."

When the door closed behind him, she flopped onto Sara's beautiful four-poster bed and pulled the comforter to her chin. She was dead tired, even though it was early in the day. Yet, despite her fatigue, her mind was active. She wondered about Jess, about the accident that had changed his life and hers, about the man he had become, and about her role in the greater scheme of things.

In her head she accepted the medical fact of amnesia. In many ways it was a relief to finally have answers. For five years she had not understood why he had simply vanished from her life. She'd been hurt. She'd been disillusioned. But deep in her heart she had never stopped loving him. She knew she never would. In her heart she only wanted to belong to him again, to be close to him again.

And now that seemed unlikely.

# FIVE

When Jess MacLaren returned to his parents' house late Tuesday afternoon, he found Brianna sitting in the den chatting companionably with his mother.

"Eager to get home?" he questioned, eyeing the luggage on the floor at her feet.

"I'm looking forward to going home," she answered truthfully.

"Mom took good care of you, I presume?"

Libby MacLaren smiled indulgently at her eldest son, as if to say, "You rascal, you know I did."

Brianna grinned at him, too. "Your mother was the perfect hostess. She hovered over me like a mother hen while I was here. I haven't eaten this well in months, but please don't let my sister know I said that. She means well, but she's not a great cook."

"You're welcome to stay with us any time you're in Boston, Brianna," Libby said. "I've enjoyed having you with us. And I especially enjoyed the rare moments when the two of us got to chat. Keep writing. And give that little fellow of yours a big hug for me."

"Thank you so much," Brianna said, reaching to give the older woman an enormous hug. "It was very kind of you to take a stranger into your home—"

"Not one of us could have turned you away, Brianna," Mac interrupted.

"I want you to know I appreciate your kindness," Brianna emphasized. "I did have a hotel room waiting for me."

"But wasn't this nicer?" Libby asked.

Brianna couldn't help but smile. "Yes, it was much, much nicer. Thank you again."

"Ready?" Mac urged, touching her possessively on the small of her back.

She shot him a quick, questioning glance.

"We have a date with a plane," he reminded her. "And traffic— Well, this is Boston."

"That's one of the reasons I'm looking forward to small-town America," she dared to tease. "After watching people drive in this city, it will be paradise at home!"

Neither Mac nor Brianna spoke much on the way to the airport. He was busy fighting his way through the streets of Boston. And Brianna was too conscious of the intense feelings she experienced each time he was close and conscious, as well, that she was leaving him to go on with her life—alone. She grimaced when it occurred to her the plane ride she dreaded would carry her away from the man she loved.

When they arrived at Logan, she picked up her ticket and checked her luggage. Afterward he suggested getting something light to eat while they waited. Brianna declined food for herself but dawdled over coffee while he had pie. Conversation remained minimal.

He finally ended the prolonged silence that hung between them.

"I've finished your book," he revealed, searching her face for reaction.

Brianna merely lifted her eyes, regarding him cautiously, uncertain how to respond. She had mixed feelings. She wanted him to like the book. Yet she was fearful if he truly understood it, if he read between the lines, she would be exposed somehow. When she spoke, she kept her remark light, bantering.

"Well, what's your verdict, counselor? Did you like it?"

He ignored her question.

"Was it difficult having your baby alone?"

"Again?" she queried, eyebrows raised. She leaned back in her seat, studying his face, memorizing every angle, every laugh line. Then she decided not to make an issue of his question, but to answer honestly. "In some ways it was much more than difficult. I don't like to remember that experience," she explained.

"I'm sorry," he murmured politely. He watched her in thoughtful silence as he sipped his coffee.

"How did you cope?" he asked. "How did you deal with your situation, Brianna? I have to confess I agree with Sara—having a baby alone seems unimaginable. I realize I may sound opinionated and judgmental again. Please don't take it that way."

She stared at him long and hard. A stranger would have absolutely no business asking these questions. But this man was not a stranger in her eyes. She took a deep, steadying breath, then, tilting her head slightly to one side, met his intense, questioning gaze head-on.

"I didn't realize I was pregnant at first. I was busy adjusting to college, adjusting to living away from my family, and adjusting to being alone—"

"Without the father, you mean?"

"Yes," she replied. "It was a very difficult period. I had to face a lot of changes in my life."

"How old were you?"

"I was a very naive eighteen-year-old."

"Did you love him?" he queried, guessing what her answer would be.

"Yes."

That one word, spoken with as much conviction as Brianna put behind it, was more answer than he actually cared to have.

"And now? Do you love him still?"

"Now and always," she responded.

"That special, huh?"

She nodded. "*More* than special."

"Did you believe he loved you?" he asked presumptuously.

Brianna delved deep into her companion's eyes, wanting desperately to find the man she had known. What she found was both familiar and unfamiliar.

In a soft but determined voice, she answered him, the lover and the stranger, as openly as she could. "He told me he loved me and I believed him. I will *always* believe he loved me."

"That's why you still wear his ring, isn't it?"

She only nodded.

He searched her face, intrigued by the emotion he read in her expressive features. When her eyes suddenly filled with tears, that inexplicable need to protect her surfaced unexpectedly. It angered him to think any man would dare hurt Brianna. Swayed by his strong feelings, he was forced to vocalize his thoughts.

"You realize I don't think much of this man of yours. You are one bright, beautiful lady. Excuse me for what I am about to say, Brianna, but that man was either a crazy fool or a damned bastard for leaving you!"

His words hit home. She glanced away quickly, hoping he wouldn't push any further. This situation was difficult enough without witnessing his reaction. She couldn't prevent the tears from falling.

As the first one slid down her cheek, he reached across the table. His thumb coaxed her chin upwards, tilting it slightly. Ever so gently he wiped the droplets from her soft skin.

When he spoke again, his low voice was filled with reverence. "I'm not sorry I said that, but I wish you wouldn't cry."

As his fingers caressed her damp cheek, Brianna sensed a powerful emotional conflict in him. She understood the look on his face. She'd seen adoring reverence before. But she was not accustomed to the puzzlement clouding his eyes. She desperately wished she could smooth away his confusion. But she was helpless.

She wanted to pull away, to distance herself. Yet, the light touch of his hand sent tingling awareness all through her. And this was not the time and place to be wanting him as much as she did.

She cast a nervous, downward glance at her wristwatch as he continued wiping her tears with tender, stroking motions.

"I have to board the plane now," she said.

There was an obvious note of reluctance in his voice

when he muttered, "Sure." He had no choice. He was well aware of that. She was going home. It was time for them to say good-bye.

Hoping the gesture appeared effortless, he rose and moved to Brianna's side, possessively reaching for her arm to steady her. He needed to touch her. As she pushed the chair in, his hand held fast to her arm. It was their only communication.

Neither of them spoke. Neither of them looked forward to this parting. And neither of them was willing to admit it.

The walk to the departure area was an emotional maelstrom for Brianna. His arm lay firmly along her waist, one hand splayed over her slim hip. She could feel his heat through her clothes, and the old, once familiar, melting sensation coursed through her, just as it always had when he touched her.

She didn't want to leave. Yet she realized in a matter of minutes she would have to bid farewell to the man she loved so deeply. And grudgingly, she accepted that the end of the walk would mean good-bye forever.

When they arrived at the designated area, his strong hands came to rest on her small shoulders, easily turning her pliant body.

"Will you be all right?" he inquired, concern evident in his deep voice and in the questing malachite eyes that slid slowly over every inch of her as if appraising her troubled features. "Didn't you tell me you hate to fly?"

She took a steadying breath and nodded hesitantly, struggling to maintain composure. Her physical response, not only to his touch, but also to the caring tone of his voice, was strong. Her desire for him was so intense she wanted nothing more than to throw herself into his arms and cling to him.

But for the moment, she controlled her physical desires.

He, on the other hand, found himself gradually succumbing to his growing need to keep Brianna close. His hands glided down her slender arms, then settled comfortably upon her tiny waist, drawing her so near their bodies were molded together.

As he watched the emotions play across Brianna's face, he noticed the pool of tears in her pale eyes. And that familiar, protective tug gripped him more powerfully.

"Please don't cry," he commanded softly, emotion edging his normally confident voice.

It was that unspoken emotion Brianna responded to. She tilted her head to peer at his dearly loved face, and without warning, his lips descended to hers, claiming them in a deep, searching kiss that went on and on. His kiss was at the same time urgent, demanding, and sweet. It left her weak with longing, yet powerless to do anything to relieve that longing.

And his hands, as they gathered her ever closer, were like a lingering memory, warming her with increasing intensity.

Slowly, and with considerable effort, he raised his head. But he did not release her. He hadn't wanted to part his lips from hers. The sharing was beautiful beyond words. He kept Brianna enfolded securely within his arms, longing to detain her until the last possible minute.

He breathed in her sweet fragrance, buried his chin in the softness of her hair, and savored the moment. Brianna's kiss sparked a fire in him that was altogether different from the affection he felt for Chris. And deep inside he realized that spark needed very little fuel before it ignited and burned out of control.

*It feels so good, so natural, to be holding her,* he thought. *I don't want to stop holding her. I feel comfortable with her even when she's quiet. She's easy to be with. . . . I don't want her to go. . . .*

A wave of regret besieged him. And then his mouth was on hers again, eagerly possessing it, claiming it as if he had the right. Deep within, feelings sprang to life, pushing him to demand more of her with his lips. He struggled to maintain some semblance of control, but a more powerful force held him. That force would not be denied.

Unwillingly, he tore his mouth from hers but kept her body pressed tightly to his own.

"I'm sorry I made you cry, Bri," he whispered, his breath warm against her ear.

She shook her head, struggling to deny the feelings that had overpowered her. Calling upon her inner strengths, she pushed herself away. She had to remember things were different now. He wasn't hers.

But no man's kisses had ever left her weak with desire, except his. No one but Jess had ever called her Bri. And this was Jess. For a moment, for just one fleeting moment, being held in his arms, being kissed by him, and hearing him call her Bri made her feel as if five years had melted away.

Yet it hadn't. Brianna was firmly entrenched in reality. She took one small step from him. Then summoning courage from deep within her reserves, she backed away uttering only a faint "Bye—"

She fled toward the doorway, calling good-bye to him in her mind. *Good-bye, my dearest one. . . .*

*Good-bye. . . . Here's your freedom. . . . Be happy. . . . Have a good life. . . . I love you. . . .*

As she stepped into the corridor, she stopped and turned toward him, needing to have one last memory to carry with her. She saw him lift his hand to wave a silent farewell.

And then she continued into the waiting plane, murmuring, "Good-bye. I love you, Jess."

Three weeks later, Luke MacLaren sauntered casually into his brother's office, scanning the large room for signs of activity. There were none.

"You know, Mac, your secretary told me you weren't busy, but she didn't say you were downright idle."

Mac had been staring out the window. Now he turned his desk chair toward Luke. "Hi" was all he said.

"Chris called this morning. She's concerned about you. The rest of us are, too. She says you've been moody and distant. She says you've been working too hard, not that I can believe it from what I see here today. She also says you've, shall we say, neglected to keep several recent dinner engagements. Chris is worried. She was reluctant to discuss your problems with me, but she's run out of alternatives. She can't seem to communicate with you.

"So she dumped her worries in my lap. She asked if there was anything I could do to help. Sounds like you're having a rough time," Luke observed, eyeing his older brother sharply. Mac was meticulously groomed, as always. But he looked awful. His face was drawn and he had deep circles under his eyes.

"When's the last time you had a full night's sleep?"

"Don't know, Luke," he mumbled.

"You want to talk about what's keeping you awake?"

He didn't respond immediately. He only shook his head, then bowed it, as if in defeat, resting his chin on his hands.

"Something's wrong, big brother," Luke continued. "You know it, even if you won't admit it. You've changed. You're snapping at everyone. You're acting bitter and resentful . . . almost as much as you did after the accident. You need help. Either talk with a professional—"

"You mean, go to another shrink?"

"Mac, I'm suggesting you seek professional help."

"Forget it. That didn't help five years ago."

"It only helps if the subject is cooperative. You weren't."

"I don't need professional help," he argued.

"Suit yourself. But . . . you do need to come to terms with whatever is gnawing at your gut."

"Sure," he replied sarcastically, "easy for you to say, Luke."

"Chris does not deserve to be treated like this. You've been giving her a bad time, Mac," he charged. "Is there someone else?"

"Someone else?"

"Don't be dense," he snapped. "Another woman? Or women?"

"No!"

"Why did you bring Brianna Dugan home?"

"She fainted. I thought she was hungry. We've been through this before, Luke."

"She's a very pretty lady."

He swallowed hard. "She is."

"And nothing happened between the two of you?"

Mac didn't answer. He just stared blankly at the wall.

And then he closed his eyes, remembering the feel of Brianna against him, the feel of her lips beneath his own.

"Mac?"

"A kiss," he confessed.

"Another?" Luke asked grinning. "You said she kissed you when she was coming to. Just that one little kiss?"

Mac glared at him. "Two," he bit out tersely. "I took her to Logan when she left for home. I kissed her good-bye."

"And?"

"It was only a kiss, dammit!"

"Home to meet the family, a few innocent, or maybe not so innocent, kisses—"

"Stop it, Luke!"

"Would you have, Mac, if you hadn't been in a busy airport? Would you have stopped with a kiss from Brianna?"

"No . . . I don't know," he admitted. "It doesn't make any difference now. . . . She's gone back home."

"Which is where?"

"Pennsylvania."

"Interesting . . ." Luke remarked.

"What?"

"You cover up beautifully, counselor. You neglected to mention the first night Brianna spent in our home. You stayed, too."

"All right," he admitted reluctantly. "I did."

"Where exactly did you stay?"

"With her."

"With Brianna? In Sara's room? There's only one bed in that room."

"So?"

"So where did you sleep?" Luke demanded.

"I spent some of the night in the boudoir chair," he hedged.

"You expect me to believe all six foot three of you slept in that chair?"

"Yes!"

"Yeah, right. Wait a minute. *Some* of the time? How about the rest?"

"I held her. She had the chills. Even extra blankets didn't help."

Luke shot him a doubtful glance.

"Nothing happened," he was quick to defend. "I didn't sleep much. I spent a large part of the night reading . . . and thinking."

"Yeah." Luke's eyebrows rose a fraction. "And you expect me to believe you held her in your arms and nothing happened?"

"She was cold. I kept her warm," he explained.

"I see," his brother remarked.

"No, you don't. You believe it's impossible not to be intimate with a woman if you're physically close."

"I didn't say that," Luke replied evenly. "What about Chris?"

"What about her? I haven't forgotten Chris."

"But you are attracted to Brianna."

"Perhaps I am," he conceded reluctantly.

"Is that what's eating at you?"

"No!" he denied vehemently. "She's gone."

"Yeah. But not forgotten," Luke mumbled. "Whatever it is you're holding inside you, it's making you a miserable son of a bitch to live with. Why don't you take some time off?" Luke suggested. "Get away from the pressures of work. Let someone else be conscientious and carry the burden. Change of scenery might, at the very least, be distracting.''

Mac showed no response at all.

In an unusual display of temper, Luke raised his voice, barking at his brother, ''You cannot continue like this!''

''And I can't escape what's in my mind by changing the scenery around me!''

''How will you know if you don't even give it a try? Go back to Eaton. Look for whatever it is you need to find!'' Luke urged.

''I went back before!'' he thundered. ''There was nothing! Remember?''

''Yeah! I remember!'' Luke's palm slapped the desk sharply. ''That was almost four years ago! You were still raging from the unfairness you felt after the accident. You didn't want to be there and you were uncomfortable when you encountered people you couldn't remember. You were so uncooperative you quit in a matter of days. Maybe now, you'd be more receptive to this confrontation with your past. You're more agitated than you've been in a while. . . .''

The look Luke fastened on his brother said it all, but Mac didn't notice.

''I'll call Steve Davidson, ask him to take us places you frequented together. Mac, are you listening to me?''

''I'm listening.''

''Well?''

''No,'' he snapped. ''I'm not—''

''I have a problem with your refusal to visit Steve,'' Luke interrupted. ''How many times during the last five years has he called and asked you to come?''

''I'm not prepared to visit Steve.''

"Yeah. You're not prepared to visit Steve . . ." he echoed harshly. "It's not that far away, you know. Only a short hop by plane. You act as if Delaware is another country or another world."

"It is!" he railed. "As far as I'm concerned Delaware is another world! Can't you get it through that impossibly thick skull of yours, Luke? I don't remember. . . . I can't remember. . . . Being with Steve and Julie makes it worse. Old friends reminisce. . . . Steve says, 'Hey, Jess, remember when we . . .' and I don't!"

"Bull! You and Steve had three long years and one terrific friendship *before* your accident. There's more to remember than there is to forget. Maybe I can't feel your frustration, big brother, but sometimes I think you use it as an excuse. Sometimes I think there's something you don't want to remember."

"There *are* a few things I'd like to forget, Luke. Waking up in the hospital hooked up to life support systems. The damn sound of those machines. The smell of the hospital room. The hell, the loneliness, the agony . . ." He ran his fingers through his thick hair. "But Steve's friendship is not on the list of things I'd like to forget. . . ."

When he made no further comment, Luke prodded him impatiently. "Well?" he repeated.

"You're going to keep nagging at me until I agree to this, aren't you? But what if it doesn't blow the cobwebs out of my memory and chase the goblins in my dreams away, little brother? What then?" he asked sarcastically.

"How ugly are these goblins?" Luke inquired, relieved he was getting through to Mac at last.

"You don't want to know. . . . Call Steve," Mac commanded.

"And you'll arrange to take vacation?"

"Yes, Luke, yes. It's obvious you won't stop hounding me unless I give in to you," he responded, his voice heavy with resignation.

After Luke left, Jess MacLaren leaned back in his chair and resumed staring sightlessly out the window. *This whole idea is futile,* he thought. *What good is any of this going to do? After five years, what's the likelihood that I'll remember anything?*

*And why does it bother me so much lately?*

# SIX

Brianna held Noah's hand tightly as she studied her shopping list. This trip into town was a necessity, but Noah wanted nothing to do with shopping. He wanted to play, to run on the beach, not follow alongside his mother in town.

"Be still, Noah," she pleaded as he tugged at her hand yet again. "Just one more store, then, I promise you, we'll be finished."

"Can we go to the park?" he asked.

"Hmm," she responded, smiling down at him. "For a little while." Even though he kept trying to dash off, she knew he was behaving as well as one could expect a four-year-old to behave.

"I wanna swing way high today," he told her. "Higher than Jenna!"

She laughed at his exuberance. "We'll see about that. Come on, the next store is around the corner."

Brianna Dugan knew the streets of Eaton like the back of her hand. She'd vacationed in the tiny seaside community since she was a small child. She felt she could move from one place to another blindfolded if necessary. Now she walked jauntily along the sidewalk, swinging hands with Noah and musing over his preoccupation with besting his cousin Jenna. She was watching him try to skip, and not paying attention to where she was going, when a large hand grasped her shoulder.

Startled, she immediately focused her attention on the man standing before her. He was a tall, broadshouldered man, with chestnut hair, smiling green eyes, and a mustache.

"Luke!" she declared, unable to disguise her surprise. "What are you doing here?"

"Brianna." He greeted her warmly. "I could ask you the same, but you did mention you vacationed here," he elaborated. "So it's safe to assume you're on vacation." He shot a quick glance at the small boy pulling on her hand. "Who's your friend?"

"My son . . ." She hesitated. Anxiety began to knot her stomach. "Noah."

"Hi, sport." Luke bent down, crouching to bring himself eye level with the child. Wide green eyes peered into his.

"My Uncle Tom calls me sport," Noah declared earnestly. "You have green eyes like me. And Mama says my daddy has green eyes, too."

"Yeah," Luke drawled, his gaze fixed on the little boy's expressive face as he chattered.

Brianna watched the exchange silently. The fleeting look of astonishment that altered Luke's expression for a moment, then disappeared, made her tighten her grip on Noah's hand. She felt her inner tension mount.

"Say, sport, how would you and your mama like an

ice cream cone? Looks to me like you've been doing some serious shopping. I'll bet you could use a break."

"Oh boy!" Noah exclaimed. "Can we, Mama? Can we, please?"

The excitement dancing in his eyes distracted Brianna from her concerns. She smiled indulgently at him as he bounced up and down at her side. Then she nodded her consent.

"Oh boy! Ice cream!" he shouted with undisguised delight.

Luke rose and straightened to his full height. "The park?" he asked.

"Hmm. Good idea. He's been begging me to take him there all morning."

"Yeah," Luke said as they began walking toward the park. "And it has benches for grown-up folks." He stole another glance at Brianna and the boy. "How've you been?"

"Fine," she replied automatically. "And you?"

"Great."

"Did your sister have her baby?"

"Not yet. She's due any day. We're all anxiously awaiting the birth—"

"Is something wrong?" Brianna ventured, sensing a change in his attitude.

"Yeah," he grumbled. "But not with Sara. Let's get the ice cream. Then we'll talk."

A few minutes later, the adults were seated on a park bench, while Noah roamed nearby, licking his ice cream cone and watching a group of older children play ball.

"He looks just like Ethan when he was small," Luke remarked suddenly. "In fact, except for the dark hair, he's a miniature of his father. The resemblance is uncanny. Looking into Noah's eyes is remarkably like looking into Mac's. You're not going to deny it, are you, Brianna?''

She was caught unprepared. For a moment she sat frozen in place, staring at him, too astounded to speak. She had never considered being in this situation and could think of no immediate response. She tried to sort through the jumble of thoughts threatening her normal good sense, tried to compose herself to speak reasonably.

Her eyes darted nervously toward Noah. He was engrossed in the ball game, unconcerned with the conversation of the adults. The sounds of children at play filled the air.

Willing herself to remain calm, she faced Luke. The family resemblance was strong. And yet, while Jess radiated authority and control, his brother appeared more casual. His eyes weren't as green or as intense as Jess's. His hair was not perfectly groomed. He was dressed in a T-shirt and ragged cutoffs. She couldn't picture Jess in anything that was not coordinated. And Brianna knew when she stood next to Luke he didn't tower over her quite as far as Jess.

''I can't deny their resemblance,'' she admitted. Reaching out, she gingerly touched her hand to Luke's forearm. ''Please don't tell Jess,'' she begged. ''I don't want him to feel responsible for something he doesn't remember. He doesn't even know me anymore.''

''Right,'' Luke murmured, nodding his head. ''You must have had a shock yourself when you ran into him in Boston.''

''I did,'' she confirmed. ''The first few times I came back to Eaton, I . . . found myself searching for him.

As time passed my hopes of ever seeing him began to fade.''

She paused, eyeing Luke as if trying to decide how much to reveal. "Then, in Boston . . . waking up in his arms was incredible—like a dream come true. I opened my eyes and there he was, looking down at me, so close. . . .''

Again she paused, this time to blink back a few unbidden tears.

"He said you kissed him," Luke remembered. "At the time, I thought it was strange.''

"Jess must have thought so, too. But there I was in his arms. And I wanted to be closer, to hang on to him so I wouldn't lose him again. I wanted to let him know, regardless of the past, I'd take him back. I didn't think it through, I simply reacted. He kissed me back and it felt like yesterday, not years.''

Her gaze met Luke's. "I got over being hurt. Having Noah helped me through. I loved your brother very deeply five years ago. And though I've no right to him, I still love him, in spite of . . . everything.''

"You've been through a great deal alone.''

"My sister lets me lean on her," she explained. "But there are times when it's not enough. . . . I'm sorry, Luke. This isn't your problem.''

"I disagree, Brianna. We were raised to believe in the strength and unity of family. Actually, Noah's a part of our family. A little while ago that threw me for a loop. The entire family is excited about the birth of the first grandchild. But you and I know Sara's baby won't be the first.'' His voice sounded husky. His eyes shifted in Noah's direction.

"I can only guess what you're feeling, Brianna," he went on, his low voice soothing. His entire demeanor reflected the comfort he offered verbally. "And I don't want you to be upset because of me. I'm feeling some mighty strong shock waves myself right now." He shifted his long frame to face her.

"I'm not just his brother, I'm his closest friend. I know the truth would hit Mac with much more force. But this isn't a situation where either of you had any control. . . ."

His hand came to rest on Brianna's shoulder. The gesture was brotherly and very reassuring.

"You should know," he went on, "I saw Noah's picture in your wallet. Mac asked me to look for your phone number. He was concerned your family might be worried." Luke shrugged apologetically. "The child seemed familiar, but I didn't figure out why until Mac came back into the room. You'd already admitted you knew him, so I thought maybe—then I thought, well, maybe not. The picture doesn't do justice to their likeness."

He fell silent, remembering a day five long years before and a small velvet box he'd found in Mac's dresser. A receipt had been tucked inside. He glanced at Brianna's left hand. The ring she wore fit the description of the diamond his brother had purchased. And she'd made a point of telling him she still loved Mac. His gaze rested thoughtfully on the mother of his brother's son.

"After the accident, I asked Mac's law partner if there was a woman in my brother's life," he continued. "Steve told me he suspected there was, but—" he broke off, shrugging again.

"I never met him. We kept to ourselves. . . ." She hesitated, then turned her pale eyes on Luke. "Can I trust you?"

"Yeah," he assured her, grinning. "I'm family. You can trust me."

Brianna sighed deeply. Her eyes sought out Noah. "He's my life, Luke. I won't ever let anything harm him. Not my past . . . Not anything," she finished fiercely.

"Okay, I understand. But, you'll let me get to know him, won't you?"

She raised her legs onto the park bench and wrapped her arms around them, unconsciously wrinkling her brow as she considered his suggestion.

"I have some reservations," she replied at last.

"I'm sure you do. Don't worry. I won't tell Mac. That's not my responsibility. The two of you have to come to terms with one another. *You* should be the one to tell him about Noah. No one else has that right. Even family members are outsiders in a situation as complicated as this.

"You know, I felt obligated to read your book," he continued. "Having met you was reason enough, but after listening to Rachel and Sara and Mom, I had no choice. Now that I've seen Noah, I realize it's essentially your own story."

He took her small hand, enfolding it carefully in his. "You're not alone anymore. If you ever need anything, any help at all with Noah, I want you to let me know."

Brianna bobbed her head several times, responding automatically to the compassion she heard in his voice and saw in his eyes.

"Would you mind if I took him fishing some morning?"

She hesitated, then realizing how much she trusted him, shot a grateful smile in his direction. "Noah would love to go fishing. He always begs to watch the fishermen at the water's edge.''

"Good. We'll go tomorrow," Luke decided, with a quick nod of his head. "And now I guess I'd better come clean.'' He smoothed his mustache with his index finger, as if he were stalling for time. "We're staying down the coast a little ways—"

"You mean Jess, too?"

"Yeah. He's been going through a difficult time, not sleeping well, not eating properly, etcetera. Since late spring— As a matter of fact, Brianna, since you were in Boston, he's been very unlike the brother we all love so much. He's restless, irritable, short-tempered. Not at all himself. Makes me wonder why—" he broke off, watching as Noah climbed onto a distant swing.

"Anyway, I badgered big brother until he agreed to try my *theory*. Now that I understand how involved your relationship was, I'm certain *you* are the catalyst in this reaction.

"He either can't or won't say what's bothering him," Luke continued. "I was hoping if he came back to the place where he spent that lost year, if he met with old acquaintances, spent time with them, it would help him remember. It's a long shot, I know. But . . . damn, it's tough to watch someone you care about struggle.''

He paused, rubbing his hand across the back of his neck.

"You know, Brianna, you just might be able to help. If you could give me suggestions—people, places, things he was involved with five years ago. Things Steve didn't share?"

"I don't—'' she began, wondering how she could

open herself up to the past when she knew how much it would hurt.

"Think about it, Brianna," he advised. "Guess I'd better get going. Mac's probably wondering where I am. How about directions to your place?"

"What?" Her thoughts had drifted back to another time, remembering, searching. "Directions?"

"Yeah, so I can take Noah fishing?"

"Oh, of course. I'm on Beach View. Go all the way to the end. Take the first left. It's the green cottage next to the dunes."

Luke rose to his feet. An infectious smile lit his face as his eyes found the child.

"Noah!" he called from the pathway. "Bye, sport! I've got to go."

The child jumped off the swing and came running toward Luke as fast as his legs would carry him. "You didn't tell me your name."

Luke chuckled as he tousled the small boy's thick hair. "My name is Luke MacLaren, but you can call me Uncle Luke."

"Uncle Luke?" Brianna's voice was clipped.

"Yeah. Mr. MacLaren is too long and formal for a little kid. Besides, Brianna, it is Uncle Luke," he emphasized quietly.

"Hmm," she responded. "So be it."

"Yeah. So be it." He winked at Noah. "How would you like to go fishing with me?"

"Fishing! In the ocean? Oh boy, can I, Mama? Can I?"

"Sure," she answered, smiling at her jubilant son.

"I'll be back tomorrow." Luke gave the child an encouraging pat on the head. "Take good care of your mama."

"Bye," Noah called as he scurried off toward the swings.

"Where will Jess be while you're fishing?" Brianna demanded, needing to know.

"I'll keep Noah away from Mac, I promise. Scout's honor. Besides, he's made plans with an old friend. They're going to roam their favorite haunts. I'm sure Steve will keep big brother occupied with people and places from his forgotten past. Any more questions?"

Her mind filled with doubts. "What do you think he'll do if, or when, he discovers he has a son?"

"I honestly don't know how he'll react. I imagine learning you're the father of a four-year-old child could be quite a shock. Don't worry about it right now, okay?"

Brianna sighed in frustration. "That's not what I meant. Do you think he would try to take Noah from me?" Her voice broke as she questioned him.

"We won't let him," he stressed, reaching to give her a reassuring hug. "You love Noah and he loves you. You are the child's security. You're the one who shares his home. You're the one who's always been there for him. Was the man you knew so cold-hearted?"

She jerked her head up. "No! He was always warm and caring."

"Did he know you were pregnant?"

His question took her by surprise, but she answered directly. "No, I didn't know myself until weeks after he was gone. It ended without warning, Luke. One day he was there . . ." She shuddered, remembering the pain of his disappearance.

"Dad had a heart attack," Luke explained. "When Mom called to tell Mac, he promised he'd be on the next plane to Boston. I guess he left Eaton in a hurry. But he never made it home from the airport," he stopped, pursing his lips thoughtfully. "I don't think you want to hear the details."

She shook her head. "No. Not now."

"I'd better go. See you tomorrow morning. Early."

"Okay," she agreed. "We'll be waiting."

Brianna watched Luke MacLaren until he veered off the path toward the narrow street. Then she focused her attention on her young son, playing happily on the swings, engrossed in a make-believe world, oblivious to the real world around him. How fortunate he was not to be burdened with the concerns of adults.

She considered what Luke had told her. He'd answered another of her questions. Jess had had good reason for leaving. But she wondered why he hadn't called, and then she struggled not to think about his accident.

Luke wanted to help. She wanted Jess to regain his memory.

But could she help? Should she? And if Jess did remember, what would happen to her, and to Noah, and the secure little world she had created for them?

This was not going to be an easy decision.

A few days later Brianna stood peering in the window of the Main Street Antique Shop. It wasn't often she had the opportunity to look in these windows. In fact, it was quite a luxury. Usually shopping trips meant dragging a reluctant Noah from store to store without stopping for extras. If it wasn't on her list, she didn't bother. Noah was much too young to endure lengthy shopping trips, so she did what she could to avoid them.

This morning she was on her own. Luke had come at dawn to take Noah fishing again. She'd finished with her list and was amusing herself looking into all the shop windows she'd never had time for previously.

"Show me what it is that put such a delighted look on your face, and I'll buy it for you," a familiar deep rumble sounded close to her ear.

She glanced over her shoulder, tossing her hair back out of her way. "What are *you* doing here?" she inquired, surprised Jess wasn't with his friend Steve.

"It's a long story, Brianna. I'll be glad to explain over lunch. First though, tell me what you liked so well in the window."

"Everything," she revealed, smiling.

"Come on, we'll go in." He grabbed her hand, and with his customary self-assurance, pulled her along into the cozy little store. The bells on the door jangled a welcome as they entered.

They browsed among the antiques for almost an hour, peeking into nooks and crannies at old pottery, glassware, and china, thoroughly enjoying themselves.

"You should see yourself, Brianna," he whispered, grinning boyishly. "Your eyes are all lit up. You look like a kid in a toy store."

She gave him an odd smile. "I'm not surprised. I feel like a kid in a toy store. There are so many lovely things, I don't know where to look next."

"Like this?" he asked, pointing to a small crystal pitcher.

"It's exquisite!" she exclaimed softly.

"It's yours. The blue is exactly the shade of your eyes."

She looked up from the pitcher, her mouth forming a small circle of surprise and delight.

Before she could protest, he touched a finger to her lips. "Shh. I want you to have it," he insisted.

When they'd had their fill of browsing, they left the cozy antique shop. His hand rested lightly but possessively on her hip as he ushered her into the bright midday sun and directed her down the street to a quaint gray building she had never noticed. In her usual haste she had mistaken the place for a residence because it truly resembled one. It appeared to be just an old Victorian-style house but for the sign hanging on the lamppost, WILMINGTON.

Stepping inside was like stepping into another era. The decor was as Victorian as the exterior of the building promised. Heavy, gaudy, and ornate beyond description. Everywhere she looked her eyes feasted on another treasured Victorian relic.

Brianna was fascinated by the atmosphere in the dining room and so engrossed in ogling the decor, she gave little thought to the auburn-haired man sitting across from her.

Eventually she realized she'd been silent. She took a sip of water and cleared her throat, preparing to face him. "What are you doing in Eaton?"

He raised his head, impaling her with an apologetic look. "I promised to tell you over lunch, didn't I?" He set his fork on his plate. "You once asked me where I studied law. I went to Temple University in Philadelphia. . . ."

The emotion she read in his somber gaze kept her still, as if she were pinned to her seat.

"Luke and I came here to visit Steve Davidson, my roommate from law school. He grew up nearby. After we graduated, we went into practice together in Lewes.

"Steve called earlier to cancel our plans because of

a family emergency and Luke was busy today, so . . . I decided to reacquaint myself with some of the local color. I was driving through town when I spotted an unforgettable mane of long sable hair crowning a petite, womanly shape I somehow suspected was yours. And the rest you know,'' he ended, smiling a sort of crooked half-smile.

She could tell from the reserve in his tone and the barely perceptible hesitancy in his speech that he was reluctant to talk about the past. Deciding not to question him further, she focused on her salad, stabbing repeatedly at the remains.

In the ensuing silence, he regarded her speculatively, first admiring her delicate beauty, then wondering about the woman beneath the porcelain doll exterior. At last he asked, ''What brought you to Eaton, Brianna? Another promotional tour?''

''No. I've rented a cottage for several months,'' she began, not quite sure what explanation to give his direct question. ''I have relatives who live close by. They suggested we might enjoy it here.''

Guilt welled up swiftly. She hated deceit, especially with Jess. But she couldn't tell him she'd been coming to Eaton since she was a child. Her mind rushed through a number of topics, searching for one that was impersonal, safe to discuss.

''Lunch was scrumptious!'' she said, grasping on to the most innocuous subject possible. ''Thank you. What more can I say?''

He sat there, his chin resting on his thumb, his index finger covering his mouth. It was obvious he was listening to her every word, but behind the intense eyes watching her so closely, he seemed to be having deep thoughts of his own.

"Say you'll spend the afternoon with me or at least say you'll walk along the beach with me," he insisted soberly.

Brianna considered his invitation. "I'd like that, but . . . You're still seeing Chris, aren't you?"

He took a long, deep breath, then exhaled little by little. "If I say yes, I spend the afternoon alone. If I say no, I'll get to share the afternoon with a beautiful lady. What do I do?" he implored, expressing out loud his inner battle.

"Just be honest," she responded, as guilt stabbed at her again.

"I'm still seeing her, but we've been having problems. No, that's not true. *I've* been having problems. *I'm* the one responsible for any difficulties Chris and I are experiencing."

Brianna knew this admission had not been easy for him. She watched as he stared blankly across the room.

"Guess you wouldn't consider keeping an unfaithful creep company, huh?" he ventured.

"Have you been unfaithful?"

"No, I haven't." *At least, not yet*, he added silently. Strong feelings for this woman washed through him again. Wave after wave battering his established principles.

"It isn't too difficult to be truthful, is it?" she challenged.

"Nooo," he responded, shaking his head. The beginnings of a smile tipped the corners of his mouth. "Being truthful is always the better choice. . . . And now it's your turn, Brianna. Do you want to spend the afternoon with me? Remember . . . truth," he reminded her, his smile spreading.

"Hmmm, truth is, I'd enjoy walking along the beach with you."

"Then enough of this talk, woman, let's go."

Later, as they walked side by side along the sandy beach, Mac studied Brianna's diminutive features. He never seemed to have his fill. Time and time again he gazed into her pale blue eyes. Yet each time felt new. The feeling was decidedly unsettling. Still he couldn't resist watching every move she made.

"I wish you could see yourself, Brianna. You are truly beautiful. Your face is glowing from the warmth of the sun, your eyes are sparkling with delight, your hair has been caressed by the wind—"

"My feet are wet and sandy," she added, playfully interrupting his effusive evaluation of her appearance. She was pleased by his flattery, but embarrassed just the same. As she sent him a tentative smile, he draped a well-muscled arm over her shoulder, and in seconds she felt his warm fingers running boldly along the side of her face.

Brianna's breath caught in her throat. Her skin tingled with sensation. His touch kindled a fire in her like the old, familiar flame that always made her melt. Dining with him had been enjoyable and she was feeling relaxed. She wanted this, wanted to be with him. And yet, she wasn't entirely comfortable with the situation. He seemed to be assuming more than he ought.

She tried to distract him. "I love the ocean. The waves pounding on the sand have a calming effect on my soul," she explained, forcing her mind and her voice to function. "That's partly why I came to Eaton." *And being here with Jess*, she thought, *feels right, almost as perfect as it was before.*

"Perhaps it's none of my business, Brianna, but I'm curious." Gentle fingers nudged her head in his direction. Intense eyes impaled her. "Where's your son? Did you bring him along this time?"

"He's with a friend for the day." Unable to ignore the impact of his stare, she forgot her fleeting resolve to keep a distance between them. She responded to his touch instinctively, reaching up to explore the fullness of his mouth with her dainty fingertips.

"Noah loves the beach as much as I do," she explained as she traced the outline of his lips.

"And this friend," he asked, "does she have children for him to play with?"

The feather-light feel of his fingers running back and forth over her neck tantalized her.

"No, the friend is a man." She swallowed hard, fighting back the desire building deep within. "He doesn't have children."

Serious, inquisitive eyes searched her face. Behind them Brianna saw questions—and anger. His touch stilled, his grip tightened slightly, possessively.

"Are you involved with this guy?"

"He's a friend."

"You didn't answer my question. Are you involved with him?" he repeated, his voice brusque.

Annoyed, she yanked away. "I did answer. He's a friend. It's none of your business anyway."

In a lightning-fast motion, he grabbed her, gathering her in his arms. He pressed her to him and held fast, his large hands gripping her tiny waist, his chin resting in a swirl of silken hair. He sucked in several deep, deliberate breaths in an effort to control the emotions racing through him like wildfire.

"I'm sorry," he murmured, his voice no more than

a faint rumble near her ear. "It seems I have a knack for making you angry."

She shifted in his arms, tilting her head to peer at his face. She opened her mouth to speak, but his lips descended, crushing the words.

Brianna felt herself slipping away. His lips were warm and wet and delicious as they slid across her mouth, masterfully drawing a response. His kiss carried her off to another time. She could hear the ocean waves pounding on the beach . . . or maybe it was the sound of her heart pounding in her chest. She didn't know or care. Her body quivered with physical awareness. He rained light kisses across her face and her eyes, then once more possessed her parted lips, this time eliciting a more fervid response.

"I needed to do that," he sighed. His voice sounded shaky yet held a hint of apology. "I keep saying things that hurt you . . . and kissing you . . . kissing you takes the hurt away." He played with a wayward strand of her long hair while he spoke.

"The first time I saw you, even before you passed out in my arms, you appeared so small and fragile I wanted to protect you . . . never let anything hurt you. Instead, I find myself pushing, making you angry."

He tucked the silken hair behind her ear. "I'm jealous of your friend and Noah's father," he confessed. "I have no right to be. . . . I don't understand these feelings. And," he blew out a long breath of air, "I'm not sure what to do about them either."

"And there's Chris," Brianna added.

Inhaling the faint scent of his cologne reminded her how different things were now. It wasn't only the scent of his cologne that had changed. Although he was much the same as she remembered—open, giving, and gentle—she sensed a subtle difference in his personality. He'd always been so sure of himself, so much in command. Today she noticed a hesitancy, a vulnerability in him she had not witnessed previously.

"Chris," he muttered. Reluctantly releasing his hold on Brianna, he turned his back, forcing himself to create a distance between them. With heavy steps he moved away, toward the lapping water. Waves threatened to wash the sand from under his feet as he stood rigid and immobile.

Only a few feet separated them physically, but an invisible wall had moved between them emotionally. He pushed his fingers through his auburn hair, making deep furrows in its thickness. Then his arms lowered to his side, in a gesture of defeat. His fists clenched.

"You make me forget Chris," he admitted. "How can I hold you in my arms like I just did, kiss you like I did, and not even think of Chris?" he demanded, shaking his head back and forth.

The anguish in his voice tore at Brianna's heart. She closed the space between them, moving swiftly to his side to offer comfort.

"Do you love her very much?" she ventured as she placed her small hand on his back to soothe him.

He stared out over the ocean. The crashing waves muted the sound of his deep voice. "I thought I did. I thought I always would."

Slowly he turned, allowing his gaze to fall on the tiny dark-haired woman standing next to him. Once more he was drawn to her, overwhelmed by something he couldn't control or begin to understand. He knew he needed to give her an explanation. She deserved that much, especially considering the way he'd kissed her.

"Everyone expects me to marry Chris. I haven't

asked her, haven't even brought the subject up. I believe marriage is forever, Brianna. It's a serious commitment. I'm not ready to make that commitment to Chris. She knows that.'' He reached out hesitantly with one large hand, gently cupping Brianna's chin, angling her upturned face to study the emotions within the depths of her eyes.

She read the look on his face and understood his confusion. It hurt to see his harrowed expression. She struggled to find something to say to ease his conscience, but the only words running through her mind at that moment were *I love you, Jess*. She knew she couldn't voice that particular thought.

''Do you believe marriage is forever, Brianna?'' His voice carried an oddly gentle tone. Intent eyes probed hers, waiting for a response.

''Y-yes,'' she replied, faltering.

''You don't sound sure.''

''It's just . . . I believe sometimes people don't have control of their feelings,'' she explained, hoping her words would lessen his frustration. ''People grow . . . people change . . . and so do their feelings. It's difficult to explain. But what I'm trying to say is, I suppose sometimes our feelings don't remain as constant as we expect.''

''Your feelings for Noah's father haven't changed since he gave you that ring, have they?''

She was startled by his question. ''No,'' she admitted.

''If he walked into your life again, do you honestly believe you'd love him as much?''

''More. I'd love him more.'' She smiled to herself, then added confidently, ''I don't merely *think* I would love him more, I *know* I would.''

"Isn't that intense, constant, forever feeling what we're supposed to take into marriage?"

"I suppose it is."

He reached out, caught her small hand, and drew her toward him. The intensity of his imploring gaze was so strong she felt as if it would bore through her.

"What about me?" he asked. "You can't deny you have some feeling for me." He gathered her slender body tenderly in his strong arms. "I'm the guy who's sharing your kisses today." Large hands cupped her bottom, urging her even closer.

Aroused by the feel of his hard body pressing against hers, she responded instinctively to his touch, wrapping her arms tightly around his waist. Her eyes never strayed from his.

"I'm not going to deny what I feel when we kiss. I'm not looking back. I've learned there's no point to that. I live in the present. You are here. You are part of right now."

She didn't get the chance to say anything further. His sun-warmed lips moved eagerly to possess hers, inciting a fire within her yet again. She yielded to his unspoken demand without thought, clinging to him as he drank his fill, giving in completely to her emotional needs, oblivious to the world outside his embrace.

The sound of laughter a short distance away alerted him to their surroundings. "We'd better start back, Bri," he said, dropping a light kiss on the tip of her nose. "I have to leave. Luke has plans to drag me somewhere for dinner."

When he mentioned his brother's name, her mind began to clear.

"I have to get back, too. I want to be home before Noah returns. I'd hate for him to find the cottage empty." She glanced at the tall man standing next to her. "I know my friend wouldn't just leave him, but he didn't expect me to be out."

"You try to be there for Noah as much as you can, don't you?"

Fully in control of her emotions once more, she answered in a lighthearted fashion, "Yup, being there comes with the job."

"I expect it does, Brianna." His handsome face was lit with amusement. His magnetic eyes held hers captive. "It sounds as if I owe you further apology for some of my past comments."

"Accepted." She couldn't keep from smiling.

"I'd like to see you again. Soon," he emphasized.

"How long are you planning to stay?"

He shrugged his shoulders. "I'm not sure. Several weeks, maybe. Luke is all fired up to help his big brother remember his wild and elusive past."

Hand in hand, they ambled along the beach. "I like living with here and now. Want to share some of it with me, Bri?"

"Maybe," she teased.

"Dinner tomorrow night." It was not a question.

"Fine," Brianna responded, distracted by the feel of his hard thigh brushing hers with each step.

*What about Noah?* she thought. *I wonder if Luke will watch him.*

"Where should I meet you?" she inquired.

"I'll pick you up."

"I'd rather meet you," she insisted. "If you tell me where and what time."

"You don't want me at your place, do you?"

"No, I don't." She raised her eyes, pleading, hoping for his understanding. "I've enjoyed today, but I think it's wrong to be spending time with you as long as you're seeing Chris. I need to set limits for myself.''

He inhaled slowly, thoughtfully. "I admire your honesty, and I suppose I understand, Brianna. . . . I can share your time on your terms. Period. That lessens the guilt you carry about dating me, right?''

She nodded her head just once. "It sounds worse when you put it that way.''

"Meet me at the Old Inn about seven," he decided. "Where did you park your car?''

"Right over there,'' she answered pointing to the biscuit-colored compact car parked at the corner they were approaching.

When she opened the door to get in, he barred the way with a well-muscled arm. As she turned to thank him for lunch, both his arms came around her, drawing her against his lean body once more. His fingers dug lightly into her slender waist.

"I'll tell you more about myself over dinner tomorrow night, Brianna. You need to understand. I don't like the restrictions you've placed on our friendship.''

"Mac—" she began.

"Shh, not now. We'll talk tomorrow.''

He bent his head, intending to brush a brief goodbye kiss over her mouth. But as he pressed his lips firmly onto her welcoming flesh, her soft lips parted to permit his thrusting tongue access to the sweetness within.

"Go,'' he groaned, reluctantly pushing her away when the first intense wave of emotion ebbed. "I'll see you tomorrow, Bri.''

"See you tomorrow, Jess,'' she responded without thinking as she started the car.

He watched her drive away, his lips fresh with the imprint of hers, his body rigid from their brief but intense exchange.

*She called me Jess again*, he mused.

# SEVEN

The drive to the inn was completed in less time than Brianna anticipated, probably because her mind was so busy with thoughts of the man she was going to meet. She knew she had to make a decision—agreeing to see him tonight had been impulsive. She knew their lives had been changed irrevocably. Yet she loved him now more than she had five years ago. Time and circumstance had nothing to do with the steadfastness of her love.

But if she decided to continue seeing him, she would be faced with ongoing problems. His relationship with Chris Whitney could not be forgotten or ignored. And there was Noah. How could she tell Jess about his child? And how could she not tell him? She knew telling him would be painful for both of them. She didn't want to hurt him, yet she couldn't keep Noah from him indefinitely.

Brianna was so wrapped up in her thoughts, she almost missed the inn, swerving into the parking lot at the very last moment.

As she parked the car she spied him standing in the gardens adjacent to the inn. She watched the tall, broad-shouldered figure leisurely surveying the roses. Her resolve weakened as her eyes slid from his dark auburn hair, over the gray suit covering his lean, muscular frame, and down the length of his powerful legs. Even with his hands slung casually in his pants pockets, he exuded an air of strength and authority.

*I'd be happy just to sit here and watch him like this,* she thought. *Or reach out to trace his brow with my fingertip and feel his thick hair beneath my hand . . . and see his eyes dancing with desire . . .*

Just as she closed the car door, he turned and smiled, and she realized, not for the first time, she'd do almost anything to see his face light up with happiness. The smiling countenance and the crinkles of pleasure framing his eyes were familiar, the same look he'd often worn when they were lovers.

She watched his eyes as he approached, saw them sweep rapidly up and down, scrutinizing her openly and frankly until the moment he stood before her.

"You look beautiful," he whispered, catching her hand to lace it with his own. He tugged her to his side, then with his free hand, trailed his fingers along the edge of her wide collar.

The tender gesture, the adoring look in his eyes, and the quiet tone of his voice were not only reminders of the past, but also indications he was experiencing an emotional tug similar to hers. Knowing this brought her a feeling of satisfaction and contentment.

But when another car door slammed, she sensed a subtle change. He seemed to shift from Jess to Mac, the proper Boston lawyer. She chided herself for even making the comparison.

"I think you'll like this place," he said. "The atmosphere is rustic, exactly what you'd expect of a hundred-year-old inn. The natives tell me the food is excellent. Are you hungry?"

She was hungry, she realized, but not for food. She was desperate to spend time with him and be close to him. The warmth of his hand incited an old need. She wanted to stretch out these moments, stealing whatever time she could.

"I'd like to see the gardens while it's still light. Before we eat? If you don't mind?"

"No objections, Bri. I was admiring the roses when you arrived," he admitted as they strolled toward the entrance of the walled garden. "Look at this brilliant vermilion rose, Tropicana. Exquisite, isn't it? Either it or the Peace rose is my personal favorite. Do you like roses, Bri?"

"Mmm, I love roses. They're my favorite flowers. The fragrance triggers beautiful memories," she answered dreamily, bending to smell one of the lovely flowers as she spoke. Then turning to face him, she continued, "Did you know there is fossil evidence of roses thirty million years ago? And the beautiful Peace rose you admire is the world's favorite rose?"

"You *do* like roses," he replied, laughing. "What kind of beautiful memories do you have?"

"Roses remind me of high school dances, birthdays, secret rendezvous . . . and Noah. Mostly happy memories," she explained, sniffing yet another fragrant bloom.

He watched the delight shining on her face. "You appear as lovely and delicate as these beautiful roses,

Bri," he observed. "What is it you were going to say, but didn't?"

"I suppose roses remind most women of their first love. . . ."

"Secret rendezvous . . . and Noah's father?" he queried.

"Hmm," she responded, sighing as she glanced toward him. "He promised me champagne and roses."

Her eyes sparkled as they met with his, then held as excitement filled the space between them.

"Why do roses remind you of Noah?" he questioned, ending their wordless exchange.

She was thoughtful for only a minute. Then she tugged on his hand, pulling him along the pathway through the garden, apparently searching all the while.

"See this rose," she began breathlessly when she'd found what she wanted. "It's called Fragrant Cloud because it's so wonderfully scented. We have one of these bushes in our yard at home. One day when Noah was much younger, he came to me crying because he'd stuck his finger with a thorn from that particular bush. He was angry because he thought it was the rose's fault he was bleeding. He called it an ugly flower. I tried to explain to him that the flower itself was very pretty, you only had to be careful not to touch the thorns. Noah was too young to understand my explanation," she remarked shrugging. "But since that day roses remind me of him."

Touching her fingers to the petals of one of the delicate flowers, Brianna went on, "I wish Noah had been old enough to understand better. Life is beautiful, like these roses. And sometimes, we encounter situations that are painful, like these thorns. But those situations shouldn't diminish the wonder of life itself."

She continued philosophizing as she ran her finger back and forth over the soft petal, "If there be thorns along our paths we may choose either to avoid them, or to touch them and deal with the consequences. Perhaps we wouldn't value the lovely rose, or life, so much if there were no thorns." She lifted her eyes to scan his face as she finished speaking.

He was watching her, his eyes filled with a mixture of wonder and respect. "In your book a very young woman sits by the ocean telling her baby daughter to treasure the precious gifts life offers us above all else. That's much the same idea."

She nodded. "Maybe that belief helps me keep my perspective." She turned away to examine another rosebush, avoiding the intensity of his searching eyes.

"I really did sit at the beach with Noah and talk to him like that," she revealed quietly. "He was just a baby. He couldn't understand what I said, but I'm sure even then he felt the love I have for him."

Mac reached out, placing his hand lightly on her shoulders, then turned her gently so he could view her face. "And, as in your book, did you tell him that his father loved him, too, even though he'd never know him?"

She could only manage to nod in reply.

"In the book your daughter's father dies before she is born. What happened to Noah's father, Brianna? Why did he leave you?"

She hesitated, shutting her eyes to conceal her feelings. For five years she'd had no idea why he'd left. Now she understood what circumstances had torn them apart, but she wasn't sure how to answer his question. And she was tired of keeping the truth from him, tired of the deceit, tired of denying Noah.

"Bri," his deep voice broke through her conflicting thoughts, "you don't have to answer. I had no business asking."

All at once he released his hold on her and took a step back, jamming both hands into his pockets. Deep furrows etched his forehead, accentuating his puzzled expression.

She saw the physical evidence of his frustration and sensed the guilt he was feeling. Knowing her own ambivalence was a contributing factor made the moment even more difficult.

But what could she do? Should she say, tactfully, but evasively, he left me to join his family? Or should she simply blurt out the truth—"You're his father, Jess." She wasn't prepared to be so blunt or so uncaring. For the time being, silence seemed the wisest choice.

"Please don't be annoyed because I didn't answer," she implored, reaching out gingerly to touch his sleeve.

"I'm annoyed with myself," he admitted as he gathered her close and planted a feathery light kiss on top of her head. "I shouldn't have asked such a personal question. Are you ready for dinner?"

"I was enjoying the garden so much I forgot about eating."

"As tiny as you are, you probably don't need to eat much," he chuckled. "Come on, let's go inside."

Once they were seated, Brianna felt the sheltered ambience of the dimly lit, rustic inn. Even though there were other tables nearby, she felt as if she were dining alone with Jess. The waitress contributed to that illusion, quickly stepping out of sight after she brought their appetizers.

"This smells wonderful," Brianna declared, inhaling the stimulating aroma of crab soup.

"Tastes even better than it smells. Try it," he coaxed, watching as she took the first tentative sip. "It's spicy—a specialty common to the coastal area."

"It's delicious! You chose this charming old inn with its lovely rose gardens. And now the soup. Are you going to be an expert on everything this evening?"

"We'd better wait until our dinner comes to make that judgment. So far it seems I've made an excellent choice." His green eyes twinkled with merriment. Then he laughed outright. "I have a confession, Brianna. My friend Steve recommended this place. We couldn't afford it when we were younger, but now . . ." He shrugged.

"Oh," she said, her amusement obvious. "That explains it. All this is not due to your charm, but to your friend's excellent taste."

"Afraid so," he admitted, a trace of laughter remaining in his voice.

As Brianna buttered a slice of warm, freshly baked bread she watched him through partially lowered lashes.

"Mac," she began on a cautious note, "is being here in Eaton helping at all?"

His eyebrows knit together as his expression grew thoughtful. He raised his hand to his thick hair and dragged his fingers through it. "I don't know. Maybe." His voice sounded serious, no hint of laughter left.

"Maybe?" she repeated.

He stared at her pensively for a few silent moments before continuing. "Steve and I have been to a lot of places I remember. Fast-food places, shopping centers, laundromats, bars, places where we fished . . ."

Brianna had no trouble recognizing his customary reluctance to touch upon the past. She felt guilty for bringing it up. The waitress's approach provided a way to avoid the subject a bit longer.

"Here's our dinner. If it doesn't taste as superb as it looks, we'll blame Steve and you're off the hook. But, I have the feeling Steve knew he was giving you good advice."

"Brianna, I agree the meal looks superb, but I have no desire to spend the evening discussing the merits of Coquilles St. Jacques and spinach salad. I'd rather explain myself," he said. "This is the perfect opportunity."

"Mac—" she began. A kind of dread welled up inside her. She knew he didn't like discussing himself or his past. She knew dredging it up would be painful. And she could see he was already tense. His posture contradicted his words.

"Brianna, listen to what I have to say. Try to understand. That's all I ask. You've put some of your life and your pain into your book," he pointed out. "That helps me understand what you're about."

"That's only part of me," she corrected softly.

"I know, Bri, believe me. You're the only one who can know the extent of your own painful experience. Other people may listen and offer their help, but they don't feel it in the same way. They can't," he stressed.

"I went to law school, as I've told you, in Philadelphia. At the time I believed the distance from home, a break from my strong family ties, would be good for me. You know, young man strikes out on his own, et cetera. I even changed my nickname. At home with my family Mac sounded like an endearment. Away from there, Mac was too impersonal, like any bum on the street without a name.

"The change was good. I learned to function independently. I came to rely on myself for everything—not parents, brothers, or sisters—only me. I wanted to prove my independence, prove my self-worth. Show the world what I, Jess MacLaren, could do without the prestige of the family name behind me. I thought I wanted to be separate from them. I *needed* to prove I was made of the same strong stuff, as determined as the first Jonas MacLaren, the one who ventured to a new country, who battled the elements and, with only God at his side, established himself as a force to be reckoned with. If he could surmount impossible odds, travel here, rise from a poor immigrant to a well-respected, wealthy member of society . . . then I could, too.

"I didn't have the inclination to follow in my father's footsteps. The first Jonas designed and built magnificent sailing vessels. My father works not only on the original site, in the original structure built by his namesake, but in the very room where those long ago designs were drawn. Luke and Ethan have inherited that innate talent. They dream designs. Sara and Rachel are artistic each in her own way as well. Andrew and I, well, we follow different drummers . . . although the love of the sea is deep within us all.

"The accident—" He paused, inhaling deeply, as if the action was needed for him to continue. "The accident forced me to reevaluate my priorities. It taught me, no, reminded me, exactly how important the strength of our family unit is. Each member, in his or her unique way, aided in my recovery, showed me what an integral part of the unit I am.

"I enjoyed living here in Eaton. The ocean, the fishing and sailing were in my blood. The things I had always done at home and could do here also, gave me pleasure. Steve and I spent quite a few weekends at his parents' home near Lewes. After spending two years in this vicinity, I decided to make it my home.''

"Eaton is such a peaceful little town. It's easy to feel as if you belong here," she agreed. "I'm sorry, you were saying?''

He sort of grunted and smiled a self-deprecating kind of smile. "I did feel as if I belonged. But I didn't, Brianna. I belonged in Boston with my family.''

"So much for independence?''

"I have my own life, separate, yet interwoven with theirs.''

"Interwoven with theirs," she murmured, remembering her brief association with the welcoming MacLaren clan. "A closely knit unit . . .'' As other memories tried to superimpose themselves, Brianna suppressed them. "Go on. I didn't mean to interrupt.''

He nodded, then continued. "Most of the last year I lived here is lost. I know I'd rented a little place in town. Steve and I were roommates in law school. He got married. I needed a place of my own. That's about as far as my memory goes. I expected the first year after school to be tough, demanding. It probably was, but I don't remember.

"The other day Luke and I returned to the street where I used to live. The trees have grown bigger. The paint is peeling off the old frame house. The total appearance is different than it was five years ago, but I recognized it.''

He halted his narrative to take a sip of wine.

"Hey, don't look so solemn," he coaxed as his gaze met with hers. "Enjoy your dinner while it's still hot.''

"It's delicious, but there's so much," she countered.

It was true, but she didn't feel much like eating either. She was completely involved with listening to his account of the past. As she watched him, she felt his frustration as keenly as if it were her own.

"Will that help?" he inquired, reaching across the small table to stab one of the scallops on her plate. A look of playful merriment lit his face. He proceeded to stab another, offering the second morsel to her. When she declined, he popped that one in his mouth also.

"You're a good listener, Bri," he observed, "and there's more I ought to explain. Of course, I'll give you equal time someday."

"Someday," she murmured, staring sightlessly at her plate, "maybe . . ." And she thought, *If I ever find the courage to discuss the way it was between us five years ago.*

She was vaguely aware of his eyes on her but hesitant to face the intensity she knew would greet her. When he spoke, she realized he'd somehow sensed her unexplained reluctance.

"Do you have room for coffee?" he inquired, cocking his head and grinning sympathetically when she glanced at him.

"Possibly."

"How about dessert?"

She smiled and shook her head. "Not a chance!"

"What if I bribe the waitress and order dessert to go? You can share it with Noah. He does like desserts, doesn't he?"

All at once she was filled with overwhelming admiration. He was unknowingly offering his own son a special treat.

"That's so thoughtful. Noah will love it. Thank you for thinking of him."

"You are most welcome, Brianna," he returned gallantly. "When are you going to introduce me? You know I'd like to meet him."

"No," she shook her head.

"I've already told you I'd like a house full of children someday. And I get along well with kids, if I do say so myself. Besides, with a mom like you," he declared, "he must be one terrific little boy."

"No," she repeated firmly. "Not yet."

"What you mean is, don't push, don't get so close. Am I right?"

"Yes," she acknowledged slowly, with difficulty.

"Why, Brianna? Why do you construct these barriers?" he implored. "At times we seem so close, almost sharing our thoughts and feelings. Then you pull away and erect fences. Don't you understand how much I want your friendship . . . and your trust?"

"You have my friendship," she insisted. "Trust . . . is difficult. It may take some time. Noah isn't accustomed to men except for Tom, my brother-in-law. I don't want him to form an attachment and be hurt when it ends."

"I wouldn't hurt him, Bri, or you. Surely you realize that," he countered.

*You already have*, she accused silently. But she couldn't say that. She knew in her heart he hadn't hurt her intentionally. For just a moment she remembered the desolation of long ago and wanted, impossibly, to deny it. She rubbed her thumb along the rim of her ring without even realizing what she was doing and watched as the waitress poured the coffee.

"Am I one of the ugly thorns you choose to have your son avoid?" he ventured when she didn't respond.

"That's not fair!" she shot back. "He's too young to understand!"

"How old is he? You haven't told me."

"Noah's four."

"Perhaps you're right not to allow men to come and go in your life," he conceded. "That's not a positive influence on a young child."

"There is no opportunity in our little town for men to come streaming in and out of my life," she explained in defense of herself.

With a curt shrug of his shoulders, he accepted her comment, then continued his interrogation. "Is your brother-in-law a good father substitute?"

"He's great with Noah."

"I envy him."

"Tom?" she queried, somewhat surprised.

"Yes, Tom. And anyone who can get close to you without coming in contact with that shield of yours."

Brianna stirred her coffee slowly, avoiding his penetrating gaze. Her eyes fixed purposely on the whirlpool her spoon created in the hot liquid.

"Perhaps we both have protective devices to hide behind," she suggested, thinking how much a deterrent his relationship with Chris Whitney presented to her.

"That's not a fair assessment of the situation," he replied, obviously annoyed and trying to control his temper. "I'd like to remember—"

"No." She cast a pleading look his way. "You misunderstood." *Oh Lord,* she thought, *what do I say to make him believe me?*

"Bri, I'm sorry . . ." His voice was filled with remorse, his eyes gentle as he responded. "Perhaps I am too sensitive about my lousy memory." He reached across the table for her hand, carefully lacing his fingers through hers. "No tears, please, no tears."

*If you hadn't touched me, I would have been fine,* she thought, helpless to prevent the rivulets of tears from coursing down her face.

"We'll leave," he suggested, squeezing her hand.

The sensitivity he displayed, combined with the tenderness in his voice, was too much. She couldn't make herself look up, but she gratefully nodded her consent.

Once outside, Brianna headed for her car.

"No you don't." Gently taking her shoulder in his firm grasp, he diverted her away from the parking lot. "We need to settle a few things."

She spun to face him, poised to do battle.

"Come on," he coaxed, wiping away the tears with a tender touch. "I remember seeing a bench in the garden."

The night was beautiful. Warm summer breezes magically enveloped them in a cocoon of serenity. The sweet scent of roses hung in the air and the full moon's soft light bathed the earth with muted brightness.

They sat hand in hand on the bench, drinking in the wonder of the summer night while Brianna regained her composure.

"Luke's plan may be working," he revealed in a tone that, although hushed, broke through the evening calm. "You questioned me about that earlier. This is difficult to explain, but I haven't tried this hard to remember since I woke up in the hospital five years ago and didn't know where I was.

"Evidently the accident that altered my life's plans was pretty gruesome. The other driver was drunk. Two people died. I was lucky to come away alive. I had a severe concussion, broken ribs, a punctured lung, and this arm is pinned together now." He moved his left arm in a circle as if working out the stiffness.

"I'm thankful for my life, Brianna, but the truth is, I resent that part of me was lost. . . . The medical term is *retrograde amnesia*. Very simply, the trauma to the brain as a result of the accident induces a loss of memory. In my case, the year preceding the accident has been obliterated. In some cases, memory returns, but as time passes, as it has for me, the chance of that happening decreases.

"Sometimes I experience a weird sensation, as if I'm about to remember. Perhaps it's just that I desperately want things to fall into place," he admitted, sighing deeply.

"Do you recall what I said about experiencing our own pain? You can't imagine how it feels being told you've met someone before and having no remembrance of them.

"I suppose, if I were honest, I'd admit I agree with Luke. All I need is the key to unlock the door to my missing year. Chris thinks I should continue as I have been, building my life on what I remember, letting go of a past I don't have. But she agreed I ought to give it another chance. In fact, she offered to come along.

"I didn't want her to come. She isn't part of that time in my life. We had quite a discussion. . . ." He paused thoughtfully, looking into Brianna's concerned eyes.

Then he hung his head, filled with regret, remembering. "We had one hell of an argument. We said horrible things to each other. I believe we even meant half the things we said—" he broke off.

The stillness of the warm summer evening blanketed

them, casting a spell, bonding them. Slowly he encircled Brianna's waist and drew her close, until she was nestled securely against his hard body.

"I haven't missed her, Brianna," he confessed. "And since I found you in Eaton yesterday, I've only wanted to be with you."

His breath was warm on her ear. He swept her hair from her shoulder and touched his mouth to her neck, trailing a series of tender kisses as light as the evening's breeze across her soft flesh.

As always, she felt the inevitable response to his touch overtaking her body. "Mac," she whispered trying to raise herself off the bench, away from him.

But she never left the reassuring circle of his arms. He was so attuned to her that he thwarted her attempted protest, levering himself upward at the same time as she did.

His hands were gentle as he cupped her face. His warm, wet lips met urgently with hers. She was unable to deny the emotions spiraling within her, unable to resist touching the softness of his thick hair with her fingers. And needing to feel more of him, she slipped her hands beneath his suit jacket to explore the length of the muscled wall of his back.

"Bri, you're making me crazy," he murmured as her hand inched upward the second time.

"Jess," she whispered, pressing her body fully against his.

And Jess responded, claiming her lips as if he were starving, dismissing proprieties, boldly thrusting his tongue into untasted corners of her mouth, eagerly learning all he possibly could in the course of one not so brief kiss. As his sanity slowly surfaced, he held her close.

"You knew me before the accident, didn't you, Bri?" he accused. When she struggled to pull out of his arms, he tightened his hold.

"You've called me Jess three times before," he remembered aloud. He held her snugly, afraid to loosen his grip even momentarily for fear she might bolt. He felt the tremors wracking her body. In a gesture filled with tenderness and concern, he reached down and pushed her hair from her eyes. His lips grazed her forehead.

"Don't you agree I have a right to know?" he asked.

"Yes," she responded meekly.

He caught her chin with one hand, staring deep into her pale blue eyes. "Yes, I have a right to know or, yes, you're part of my elusive past?"

"Both," she answered.

"Will you tell me about it?"

She wished he wouldn't ask this of her. "Not now, not tonight," she put him off.

"After what I've told you this evening, I can't understand your reluctance, Brianna. Didn't you understand what I was saying? Don't you realize how much I need to fill in the empty spaces?" he implored, anger and frustration rushing, unchecked, to the surface.

"I understand, Jess. I want to help, but I can't unlock your memory," she answered, her reply weighted with emotion. "This isn't the time or place to discuss the past. . . . And I need to go home." She twisted free of his arms unexpectedly and backed away, then turned and fled.

*Please, Jess, let it be,* she prayed silently as she hurried toward her car. How much longer could she hide the truth about their past? And the truth about

Noah? Each personal question he asked brought him closer to the truth.

She found no joy in withholding his son when family meant so much to him. And if the importance hadn't been clear from the time they met again in Boston, he'd certainly made it clear this evening. He'd probably move those proverbial mountains to bring his son into that close family unit and keep him there.

She knew he had the right to know about Noah and to know what she had been to him. But she couldn't gamble with Noah's future. She would not jeopardize his happiness. There was still the possibility that Jess would not accept the truth. Her own family hadn't. She couldn't deal with that much hurt again.

It was best to remember she'd made a new life. She loved Jess. She always would. But Noah came first. She'd settle for memories of the way she and Jess used to be. At least she had that. It would be easier if he never knew how much he had really lost. She loved him far too much to cause him more pain.

As she approached her car, she rooted through her purse for her car keys. *Please let it be, Jess,* she repeated.

For a fraction of an instant he stood like a statue, watching her. Then reaction set in. He followed swiftly on her heels, his long legs closing the gap between them with ease. "This isn't over, Brianna," he stated impatiently. "We'll talk tomorrow. Or next week, whenever we're both ready."

She nodded before entering her car, and then she swung the car door shut.

Jess stiffened. The sound wasn't a slam but seemed to carry its own finality. It drove the point home. Hard. She'd refused to open up to him.

He felt angry, confused, out of control—almost as if he were watching his own life unfold in slow motion. By the time he realized she was leaving, he saw only the red glow of the taillights moving out of the parking lot.

In three long strides he was at his own car, fumbling with the lock in the darkened parking lot, frantic to follow her.

# EIGHT

She slipped into the cottage careful not to make a sound. Luke was asleep, stretched out lengthwise on the living room couch. When she entered the room, he stirred.

"What time is it?" he grumbled, opening one eye to peek at her.

"It's very late," she answered, hedging his question.

He propped himself up on an elbow and lifted slumber-filled eyes to study her. "Must've been some dinner," he commented dryly.

"Dinner was superb!" she responded.

"Looks like you were dessert."

"Luke!"

"Brianna, I'm half asleep, and it's obvious, even in my present stupor, that you have been expertly kissed."

"Luke—" she began indignantly, "I—"

"Go look in the mirror. I'm too tired to argue."

"Nobody asked you to comment on my appearance."

"I call 'em as I see 'em, and it's plain to see you

have been well kissed and are, in fact, still glowing from the effects. Now, lady, do you mind if I resume sleeping?''

She regarded the tall, sleepy figure for only a moment. ''Was Noah any trouble?''

''No, Noah was not any trouble. He's a great kid. Maybe a little lively, but still number one in my book.''

''Thanks for helping with him. You know how much I—''

''No speeches, Brianna. Go to bed. Read a book or something. Promise me you'll try to get some sleep.'' He shook his head wearily as he studied her. ''How can anybody be so darn bright and cheerful in the middle of the night?'' As he flopped back onto the couch, he begged, ''Please let me go back to sleep?''

''Here?'' she asked in surprise.

''Yeah,'' he drawled, ''here. I was doing a fine job of sleeping before you came home. If I close my eyes right now, I'll be sleeping like a baby in no time.''

''Suit yourself,'' she returned. ''You don't look very comfortable, though. And there is an extra bed—''

''I'm closing my eyes,'' he announced. ''Go to bed, Brianna. Sweet dreams.''

She watched as he grinned devilishly, then promptly closed his eyes.

''Good night, Luke,'' she murmured. ''And thanks again.''

While her nighttime routine took her through the small cottage switching lights off, her mind raced through the events of the evening. She stopped in Noah's room to straighten his covers and kiss him good night, but as she stood silently watching her precious child sleep, an echo of his father's voice reverberated in her head.

He had a right to know about their past. If circumstances had been different, it wouldn't be an issue. But it was, and her emotional tug of war continued. She didn't know how to tell him, how to smooth the way, or even if she should.

Eventually she found her way into her own room, slipped out of her clothes and into her nightgown, then crawled into bed. As she closed her eyes, she realized Jess's masculine smell had stayed with her and lingered on her, filling her senses. She breathed in deeply, then whispered into the darkness, "Good night, Jess. I love you."

The unexpected sound of Noah's cheerful greeting jolted Brianna from a peaceful slumber the next morning.

"Morning, Mama! How come you're still sleeping?" he wanted to know.

She opened her eyes, slowly focusing on her spirited young son, whose bouncing caused the bed to quake beneath her. Usually she awakened long before he did. This morning was a different story. Before she could murmur a word, his lively interrogation continued.

"I was watching you. You look funny sleeping. Were you just pretending?"

"I was sleeping until you jumped on the bed," she explained.

"Well, you were talking while you were sleeping. Can people do that?"

"Mmm hmm. What did I say?"

"I dunno. Who's Jess? You said something to Jess."

"Jess is, uh, a friend of mine. I guess I must have been talking to him in my dreams. Okay?"

"Uncle Luke made me breakfast," Noah responded,

ignoring her explanation. "I was real hungry. Uncle Luke slept here. And we watched TV together. Is it okay that I ate breakfast without you? Uncle Luke asked me if I was hungry and I was. Are you ever gettin' up, Mama?"

"Yes, Noah, I'll get up just as soon as you move off my covers," she replied, trying to hide her amusement at his exuberance. "But first, come here and give me a big hug."

He wiggled toward her and wrapped his little arms around her, squeezing her in a way that was his imitation of a bear hug. As she hugged back, she pushed his thick, dark hair from his forehead and brushed her fingers across his soft, warm cheeks.

"Mama! Uncle Luke took me out for pizza," his eyes grew wide with excitement. "And he bought me a new book. And he read me stories."

"He did?" She smiled as she touched her finger to his nose. "Sounds like you guys had a special time last night."

"We played cars, too," Noah added suddenly. "Uncle Luke says he's got bunches of little cars like mine. It's his collection."

"Kind of like your neat stuff?"

"Uh uh. My neat stuff's better than bunches of cars 'cause it's different."

"You're probably right," she agreed. "Lots of boys have cars."

"Betcha they're not as neat as Uncle Luke's."

"Betcha you're right," she shot back, grinning at him.

"Uncle Luke said he'd show me sometime. 'Cept we hafta go to . . ." His little eyebrows bunched together. "Where's he live?"

"Boston, sweetie. He lives in Boston, Massachusetts."

"Yeah. That's where. Can we go there?"

Brianna sighed and forced a smile. "Maybe some-day, Noah. I can't make a promise, though."

His gleeful expression disappeared.

"I'm sorry," she explained. "You know there are some things grown-ups can't promise."

"I know," he said sounding dejected. "Can Uncle Luke come to our house?"

She nodded. "Sure. And I promise I'll invite him. Better?"

"Thanks, Mama!" Noah hugged her tightly. "Thanks, bunches. Are you gonna get up now? I'll move off the covers." He scrambled from the bed quick as a flash. Once his feet hit the floor he whirled around and grabbed her hand. "Come on, Mama, I'll help you up." He tugged as hard as he could, struggling for all he was worth to pull her to her feet.

"Wait," she laughed, as she managed to sit on the edge of the bed. "Give me a minute, sweetheart. I'll get up by myself."

Obediently, he backed off, wide green eyes curious as she wrapped herself in her long robe, then reached for her hairbrush.

"Why don't you ask Uncle Luke to make some cof-fee?" she suggested, noting her small son's interest in her languid movements. "I'll only be a minute longer. I promise."

As he left the room, Brianna sat down on the mat-tress. Hard. She loved him so much. She'd do anything to keep him safe and happy. And she hated disappoint-ing him.

But there was no way she could promise him a trip to Boston.

He seemed to be thriving on the attention Luke lavished on him. She didn't object. In fact, she was pleased with their relationship, especially pleased because Luke had accepted the child as family. She wondered how Jess would react, wondered if he would be as accepting as Luke.

In her heart that was what she wanted most. The dream she'd held on to for years. The three of them a loving family.

But it was only a dream. In the light of day, she'd always accepted it for what it was. She'd lived through the agony of a shattered dream five years ago. She'd gone forward without the man she loved, made a life for herself and her child. Now was not the time to be dreaming of "if onlys."

She rose from the bed and, with renewed determination in her step, walked toward the closet to get her clothes.

Brianna found Luke outside, sprawled in a beach chair, watching Noah play in the damp sand near the high-tide line.

"Sorry I slept so late," she mouthed as she seated herself next to him.

"No problem. I didn't expect to see you this soon."

"Noah woke me."

"Must have had my back turned," Luke explained, with an apologetic shrug. "He's been on my heels all morning, rattling on and on about his cousin Jenna coming to visit. Seems he can't wait to show her all the fascinating new additions to his collection of neat stuff. And he thinks he can swing higher. He says he's been practicing every day in the park."

"He has," she replied. Her eyes sought out her son.

As her fingers curled around her coffee cup, she watched him making lines in the sand with his toes.

"The kid never slows down," Luke remarked as Noah hopped into the middle of a circle he'd drawn. "He's a dynamo!"

"Believe me, I realized that about three years ago."

"Yeah," Luke murmured. "So how'd your date with big brother go?"

"I knew you'd get to that," she said smiling.

"I'm glad you had dinner with him, Brianna. Having you around might help him remember. I want him to be whole as well as happy. You know, it's possible his attraction to you is linked to the past. It may be diffi-cult, even painful, for him to remember you, but in the end, he'll be able to make decisions about his future with nothing clouding his judgment."

"I don't want to tell him, Luke," she explained, her voice serious. "I want him to remember on his own. If and when he remembers me, I want it to come from him. Do you understand?"

"Yeah, all right," he conceded. "In the meantime, though, I think he needs you, Brianna. And you want to be with him, don't you?"

"Yes, but, I feel . . ." She thought for a moment. "I feel guilty . . . like the *other* woman. Yet, I can't forget what we shared, or how his love changed my life. It's all so confusing. Sometimes I wish desperately we were still together. Then I remember there's some-one else in his life now."

"Brianna, I like Chris. But last night, as tired as I was when you came home, I could see the love you feel for him written all over you. I can't say your love is wrong and Chris's love is right. And I don't think you should feel guilty. I want what's best for him. That's what you want, too, isn't it?"

"I want him to be happy. I don't want to cause more pain." She turned toward him, her inner conflict showing plainly on her face and in the pleading look she cast at him.

"This is so frustrating, Luke. Sometimes I think I should just blurt out the truth, *Jess, we have a little boy.* That seems right. And so simple. I've always preferred the direct approach. Honesty. It *seems* simple enough.

"But then I think of Jess, the whole person. I can't burden him with any more. This situation is unfair, from my perspective and from his. I can't find easy answers or solutions. And I can't simply blurt out the truth. Jess would insist upon 'doing the right thing.' In his eyes, and I'll be honest, in my eyes, too, the right thing is marriage.

"But is marriage right for us? He doesn't know me anymore. I will not force him to marry a virtual stranger. And chemistry is not a basis for marriage. We had a deep, loving relationship. Noah was created from the depths of that relationship. Besides I can't deny reality. There's another woman in his life. He consciously chose her. I can't interfere."

Her eyes sought out Noah and lingered on the child at play.

"I'd like to share my life and my dreams with him as I did five years ago. But I do not intend to force a relationship on him that's based on something he doesn't remember.

"I know it's selfish, Luke, but I want his love. . . ." she broke off, sighing heavily. "*I need his love.* I don't want to play let's pretend games. I don't want Jess assuming the role of father and husband out of a sense of duty. I couldn't live like that! Either he returns my love or we go our separate ways—''

"Your son deserves to know his father," Luke pointed out. "Isn't that worth whatever it costs?"

"I agree with you," she hedged. "But I will not use Noah! Last night Jess asked when he could meet him."

Luke's eyebrows raised in question. "What did you tell him?"

"I put him off. What else could I do?"

"If he sees Noah . . ." Luke stared into his empty coffee cup. "He'll know he's his son."

"And he *will* be hurt."

"Yeah."

"I can't hide Noah. He's part of me. If Jess wants to be part of my life, then, at some point, he'll have to meet Noah."

"You've been calling him Jess quite naturally," Luke observed.

"I know. It just slips out." She shrugged dismissively.

"Better watch yourself or he'll catch on."

"It's too late for that. He already knows."

"Yeah? How? When?"

"How do you think? I slipped up again," she admitted. "Last evening he chose to point out my mistake."

"What did you tell him?"

"That I wasn't ready to discuss the past."

"How did he take it?"

"Not well."

"Do you think he wants to be part of your life again?"

"I don't know," Brianna answered, sounding confused and unsure.

"If anyone can make him remember, it's you," Luke insisted. "Your relationship, your love . . . if it was as special as I suspect, then you're the one who's most likely to reach him."

She closed her eyes for just a moment and said a silent prayer. "I'd like to believe in the healing power of love, Luke, but . . . I can't change what happened. I can't make him remember."

"What if we try to repeat his routine?"

"Okay." She bobbed her head. "But we have to accept that five years have passed."

"Yeah. But he's worth it."

Brianna returned the grin that spread slowly across Luke's face. "He used to jog along the beach near his apartment every morning before he went to work," she said. "There's a kind of a cove about a mile and a half north. It's . . . out of the way. Not many people go there."

"But you did?"

"Every day. We were wrapped in our own little world, Luke. We didn't vary our routine much, and we didn't include anyone else in our world."

Her voice, softer than usual, spoke volumes more than the words themselves. It was obvious she was remembering details of her life that had long been buried. And just as obvious that recalling them was bittersweet.

"Sounds like a very private relationship," Luke said.

She raised her eyelids slowly, as if they were weighted. He was watching her, expecting a response.

"It was."

"And very serious?"

"What are you asking, Luke?" She stared at him, puzzled by his subtle change in attitude. "You want something, don't you?"

"Yeah. I want exactly what you want, Brianna. I want him to remember you, the past, what was between you. I want him to have his whole life back!"

Tears filled her eyes before she could do anything to prevent them. She glanced toward Noah. "That's impossible."

"Will you show me where this cove is? We'll take Noah."

"No." She refused with an emphatic shake of her head. "No, Luke. I won't go to the cove." Looking away, she blinked back the tears that now threatened with a vengeance. "You'll have to find it yourself. There are too many memories in the cove."

"I wish I didn't have to involve you, Brianna. I know this is rough. But I'm trying to do what I believe is right for Mac."

"I understand your motives. I'm just confused. I'm concerned about Jess . . . and Noah as well. How can I offer help or advice to anyone when I can't even decide what's right for me? Or my son? There aren't any easy answers to this dilemma. We'll each have to do what we feel is right and hope for the best."

"Whatever it may be."

"Luke." Brianna tensed suddenly. She straightened in her chair, staring at the jogger off in the distance. "Isn't that Jess?"

"Yeah. None other."

"Noah," she breathed.

"Relax," he advised calmly. "I'll keep big brother away from Noah."

"How?"

"Trust me," Luke suggested, winking at her.

"What if . . ." she began.

"Just smile. Distract him. Take him for a walk,"

Luke instructed. "I'll handle Noah. We'll go searching for new treasures. You deal with Mac."

"But—"

"Brianna, what's the worst that could happen?" Luke challenged.

"That's what I'm afraid of," she whispered.

"Yeah, right," he muttered. "Relax, if you can. He's seen us . . . and he looks madder than hell!"

# NINE

Jess MacLaren's looming presence cast a long shadow across the sand. He fastened a hard stare on his brother. "You two seem quite comfortable together. Have I been playing the fool?"

"Nope," Luke was quick to respond. "We're merely enjoying a friendly chat."

"Right," Jess muttered, raking his fingers through his thick hair. "Can we talk, Brianna?" His deep voice vibrated with agitation. "You and I? If Luke will excuse us?"

"Yeah, no problem," Luke supplied, rising slowly from the sand. "I've got something to do."

Forcing herself to act bright and cheerful, Brianna hastened to her feet, too. "We can walk along the beach," she suggested, extending her hand.

"Sure" was all he said. But he was quick to accept her hand and equally quick to assert his claim, pulling her possessively to his side.

Determined to keep him away from Noah, she

headed toward the water, not giving Jess a chance to choose their direction. The last thing she needed was for him to discover Noah while he was in such an agitated state. But, being Jess, he was not inclined to permit her to maintain control. Once they neared the breaking waves, he set the pace and she did her best to keep up.

As he propelled her swiftly along the wet sand, Brianna studied him, sneaking glances at the hard-set expression on his handsome face, the deep-furrowed brows, and the stern line of his jaw. This side of him was not familiar. The unusual rigidity of his posture made it that much more obvious he was in no mood for explanations or arguments.

Several minutes passed in silence. And then he queried gruffly, "What's going on, Bri?"

"Nothing's going on," she tried to assure him.

"Truth," he begged, sounding anxious.

Her fingers tightened deliberately on his. "That is the truth. Luke baby-sat for me last night."

"He baby-sat?"

"Hmm." She bobbed her head. "So I could have dinner with you."

"And this morning? What's his excuse this morning?" he demanded.

"He watched Noah while I slept late." She risked a peek at him, wondering how he was taking this news.

"I see," he muttered. "While I'm half crazy wanting to be with you, you're chatting comfortably with my brother!" And then he stopped without warning and tugged her close to him. She felt the warmth of his breath when he spoke. "Where did he sleep?"

"He slept on the couch," she insisted. "It was late when I returned. He was trying to be helpful."

"Helpful?" he scoffed.

"Yes," she emphasized, looking up at the deep frown that creased his forehead. "Jess?"

"What?"

"Why are you acting so . . ." She searched for the right word. "So beastly?"

"Because I just found you sitting cozily on the beach with Luke! Because I've been unable to close my eyes . . . wanting you!" he confessed. "I couldn't sleep, Bri."

The emotion behind his words reached deep inside her. She realized something more than Luke's presence had triggered this morning's black mood—something strong enough to affect his customary control.

She cast a thoughtful glance at the stern face that hid some unseen, unnamed hurt and wondered what to do. "Truce, Jess?" she suggested.

Sighing deeply, he dragged his fingers through his hair again. "I'm a bear this morning, huh?"

She heard the change in his voice. It was quieter now, no more than a low rumble against the crash of the incessant waves.

"Mmm hmm, you are. A MacLaren jealous of his own brother?"

He shrugged and shook his head. "Guess I have to take it out on somebody."

"Talk to me," she implored, touching his shirt with her fingertips. "Tell me what it is that's made you angry."

He pulled away then, stepping out of her reach, putting emotional and physical distance between them. A few tense minutes passed before he began to speak.

"I followed you home last night. After you'd gone inside, I felt empty . . . as if something was missing or I was only half a person. It was the same as after the accident.'' He paused, rubbing his large hand against the back of his neck.

Brianna heaved a silent sigh. Her feminine wiles had worked. The storm of anger was passing.

"I remember . . . ." he said, "feeling like a pawn in the hands of a giant, feeling like he'd picked me up and moved me back to square number one. The giant says MacLaren has to begin again. . . .

"I took it hard, Brianna. I'd lost a year of my memory. Only time. Yet, I felt as if I'd lost more. . . . I've never been able to explain those feelings, but sometimes they haunt me. Last night was one of those times. I felt empty—as if some part of me was . . . just out of my reach. . . ." For a moment he appeared lost in thought. Then he released a long, slow breath.

"Anyway, I returned to the motel. The room felt like a prison cell. So I left. I jogged along the beach for miles." He swallowed hard. "It must have been almost dawn before I went back. I paced, then I sat alone and drank. That isn't normal, but I couldn't relax. I had to do something. I tried to sleep, but I couldn't. Even my thoughts were incoherent."

She listened to every word, observed every nuance. The sunlight glistened in his hair, but her eyes swept quickly past, carefully regarding his total appearance. He stood as he had several days earlier, his back to her as he stared over the water. Instead of self-assurance, Brianna saw dejection. His hands were balled into tight fists, his broad shoulders slumped, his head hung over his chest. This wasn't the same laughing, confident man she'd loved years before. But then, she had changed with the passing of time, too.

"I did a great deal of thinking last night, Brianna,"

he continued, "trying to arrive at some decision about what to do with my life, what to do about Chris, and you, and my law practice.

"I'd like to spend more time in Eaton. I'd forgotten how much I enjoyed living here. Perhaps if I stayed for a while, made more of an effort to confront the past, my lost memories would return. Perhaps Luke is right. Or, perhaps I'm chasing dreams and none of what I've lost can ever be regained. I won't know unless I give it my best shot.

"The law firm will function without me. I'll have to go to Boston for a few days to tie up loose ends with my uncle and to talk with Chris. . . ." His deep voice dropped so that it was barely audible.

"I can't continue my relationship with her." He turned the full length of his body to face Brianna but came no closer. "You must already know that." Serious eyes searched her face, studying her critically.

"What's between you and me isn't a passing romance. It's much more. I've fallen in love with you. I need to tell Chris."

He paused, malachite eyes locked with azure blue. Time hung suspended. The sounds of the ocean waves washed over them. A sea gull cried overhead. Moments later he began to speak again.

"This morning, after a long night of soul searching, I thought I'd come to an understanding of your position. I decided you were right in refusing to tell me about our past friendship. I'd only want to know more. And, in the end, I might not be able to distinguish between what you tell me and what I remember, assuming that I will remember."

He crossed the sand to stand before Brianna. His large frame towered over her petite body. With surprising tenderness he placed his hands on her small shoulders.

"Look at me, Bri," he commanded quietly.

Her eyes lifted to meet his adoring, warm gaze and were held in an immeasurable silent embrace.

"Did I read you wrong? Am I mistaken?" he rasped. "You keep your distance from me and you cozy up to Luke. You won't introduce me to Noah, but Luke baby-sits for him. It doesn't make sense. I thought in the light of day everything would fall into place. When I came out to jog this morning, I was certain all I had to do was see you and everything would be fine. . . . Great. And now . . ." he shrugged, still impaling her with the intensity of his stare.

"Does any of this make sense to you?" His voice rose in frustration. "Does it?"

She shook her head. Dark curls swayed back and forth. Pale eyes remained locked steadfastly on green.

"Luke's a friend, Jess. Nothing more. He knows I've been confused about seeing you, spending time with you—"

"I told you I plan to end my relationship with Chris."

"This morning, Jess. Until now . . . I've been guilty of—"

"Nothing, Brianna. You're not one damn bit guilty. I am! I admit that. I need to end a friendship. I've put it off too long. I should have done it weeks ago. Now I need, just as badly, to have time with you. And I sure as hell don't need any competition from my own brother!"

She heaved an exasperated sigh. "Please understand, Jess, he isn't competing with you. I like Luke. We have a common bond. We both care deeply for you.

He thought I could help you remember," she revealed. "He's been concerned about your moodiness. He only wants to do whatever is necessary to help."

"By spending time with you?"

"Jess," she scolded.

"All right," he conceded several moments later. "I believe you. After all, if you can't trust your brother—"

"Exactly," she murmured, feeling relieved by his change in attitude. "I trust him."

"Oh, great."

She laughed then, amused by his uncharacteristic childlike look. "Maybe I trust you, too."

"Enough to introduce me to your son?"

Sobering all at once, Brianna hedged. "Why don't we work on improving our relationship first?"

He studied her, his eyes probing every line of her face. She appeared so lovely, so innocent, so guileless.

"Barriers, Bri?" he asked huskily.

Her response surprised him. She stretched to her tiptoes and pulled his head toward her, pressing her lips to his, sharing herself without restraint. The feel of her body molded to his, the gentle touch of her fingers gliding over his back, the taste of her sweet lips were proof enough.

Whatever she was trying to show him with her actions, he believed her. If she was trying to tell him, wordlessly, that she trusted him on some level, he had no doubt.

When at last she eased away, he drew her back instantly, possessively, against his hardness.

"Let's start with us," she whispered. "Just us."

He nodded in agreement. He couldn't argue with her persuasiveness. "We'll do it your way. For now."

"Trust me," she entreated.

"That's the problem. I do trust you, Brianna. Perhaps more than I should."

"No," she denied. "We need to start somewhere. Admitting you trust me, even though I've kept some of myself in reserve, is a good start."

"Perhaps it is," he murmured. He reached out to trail his fingers along her cheekbone, delighting in the softness of her warm flesh beneath his fingertips. Then, for the first time that morning, he smiled.

"I like holding you close and touching you," he confessed.

"Hmm," she agreed, "but maybe we should walk, instead of making a spectacle of ourselves."

She felt him nod, then felt fingers of air wrapping around her where only moments before she'd been pressed against him. He didn't, however, entirely relinquish possession. As they began to walk, she was drawn snugly to his side.

"I want to make a deal with you, Brianna," he informed her, as if he'd just made a monumental decision. "I don't remember knowing you. I regret that, but I can't apologize for something I've no control over. To the best of my knowledge, the incident in Boston was the beginning of our friendship. Now, here's the zinger. I will solemnly promise not to question you about our past and, of course, not to push you too hard, if you'll agree to consider our friendship as brand new. Then we can take if from right here and right now. Just us."

She shot him a quizzical look that couldn't begin to reflect the gamut of emotions sweeping through her. Starting over was impossible. She would never forget what they had meant to each other. Even if she didn't have Noah as a constant reminder, their love could not be forgotten.

"Exactly what are you asking of me?" she queried.

"I'd like you to pretend you met me recently, Bri," he explained, running his large hands up and down her arms. "Can you do that?" He planted a soft kiss on her forehead. "Will you do that for us?"

Brianna shook her head. "I don't know, Jess." She toyed nervously with the front of the T-shirt he was wearing. "You want me to forget I knew you five years ago? To pretend I just met you last month?"

"Right."

"Do I get some time to think about this?" she asked, remembering how focused they had been on each other and how deeply in love they had been.

"Sure." His hands roamed over her back, smoothing imaginary wrinkles in the fabric of her lightweight blouse.

She responded to his caressing gesture without thinking, winding her arms around his waist. Although she longed to urge him closer, to lay her head on his chest, she resisted. Instead she reached out to trace the curve of his eyebrow with her fingertip. "How much time?"

"Until I finish kissing you?" he whispered as his lips closed deliberately over hers.

She never had a chance to answer his question, only to respond to his impassioned kisses. When he began to nibble on her earlobe she managed to murmur, "Jess, there are people on the beach. . . ."

Her soft voice brought him almost back to reality. He leaned back, gazing at her like a star-struck kid. "Bri," he said, his voice choked with emotion, "you have the most beautiful eyes I've ever seen. I could lose myself staring into their pale depths.'' His lips just touched upon each eyelid in a gesture of adoration.

"Jess,'' she murmured, barely aware of anything but the feel of his warm lips caressing her as they journeyed across her face and neck. "One of us has to end this.''

"Not me.'' His mouth traveled back to the sensitive area near her ear.

"Oh Jess, please,'' she pleaded.

"More, Bri?'' he teased, smothering her words as he took possession of her mouth once more.

His kiss was urgent and all too intimate. When his hold on her loosened, she eased away. "No more. We have an audience, remember?''

A deep, frustrated sigh escaped him. "How could I possibly forget.'' He extended his hand to cup her chin. "Do we have an agreement, Bri?''

"Yes, we have an agreement. We'll take it from here and now as you say. Just us,'' she echoed, wondering how she could possibly play this charade. "Please try to understand, I *need* more time. . . .

"I promise not to push. I'll try to give you the time you need. But, I have to be honest, I can't understand why you don't want me to meet Noah. That seems to be the normal progression of a relationship.''

"I don't mean to hurt you,'' she whispered.

In the space of a heartbeat he enfolded her in his arms once again. "It's okay, we'll work it out,'' he assured her. Involuntarily his hands tightened on her soft flesh. He rested his chin in her silky hair, enjoying the feel of it tickling his skin. And then he breathed in her sweet, subtle fragrance and felt a wave of contentment wash over him. He knew he needed this woman, knew he'd do anything to keep her close.

"As much as I'd prefer to stay like this, we'd better

turn around, Brianna.'' Reaching down, he linked their hands together and turned back toward Brianna's cottage. His steps were deliberately slow, measured, as he matched his stride to hers.

"I've enjoyed our walk," she admitted.

"So have I, Bri. So have I . . ." He smiled down at her. "And we enjoyed ourselves browsing in the antique shop, didn't we?"

"Definitely."

"You liked the Wilmington, didn't you?"

"Hmm," she agreed. "I did."

"And you liked the Old Inn?"

Brianna laughed. "You know I did."

"Seems we, too, have common ground, Brianna."

"You'll get no argument from me," she returned. "I have a weakness for yesterday's treasures."

"Perhaps next week—" he began, then stopped mid-sentence. He realized in fairness to Brianna, he had to sever present ties before he could concentrate on the future. "I have to go back to Boston, Bri. I need to explain to Chris. She deserves that much."

Brianna's chin rose ever so slightly. The movement was almost imperceptible but didn't escape his close scrutiny.

"You do what you have to do," she said.

"And?"

Brianna shrugged. "I'm not sure what you expect me to say."

He stopped walking abruptly, bringing her to a halt at the same time.

"Damn!" he exploded. "I think I deserve more than passive acceptance. I need understanding. Normally that magnificent calm of yours is enviable. Right now, though, I'd like you to share what you're feeling. An invisible wall went up between us when I mentioned Chris.'' He shoved the fingers of his free hand through his hair, making deep furrows.

"You do that every time, Brianna. I know I'm hurting you. But I'm hurting Chris, too. Everyone expects us to get married. You know that.

"But, we've been arguing for weeks. We never used to disagree about anything. Now everything is fair game. I'm responsible. I'm the instigator of the arguments. Our relationship has been deteriorating, slowly, but nonetheless, deteriorating. You and I . . . my feelings . . . this relationship merely adds fuel to the fire. It's important you understand, Bri. I want you to know how I feel. You were the one who said sometimes feelings don't remain constant. People change. We don't always have control. For whatever reason, I've lost control. I don't know why or how, I only know what I feel.

"I'm hurting you and Chris. I'm responsible for causing you pain and creating this uncomfortable situation—by losing control of my feelings and allowing this to happen.''

"No," she insisted. "I shouldn't have let it go this far either.''

"You aren't to blame!" he thundered. "I'm the one making mistakes right and left. I'm the one whose life has gone haywire. You're innocent.''

"Innocent? I didn't resist your kisses last night. I kissed you back—willingly.''

"That's exactly my point. I kissed you. You kissed me." His hand tightened possessively on hers. "I wanted more. Until I break clean from Chris, I shouldn't ask for more.''

"But—" When she tried to interrupt, his quelling look stopped her.

"I need to be completely free, Brianna. Free to hold you, kiss you, love you, without guilt." Gentle fingers glided inch by inch along her spine, urging her body toward his. "Each time I look in your eyes, Bri, I see so much more than you'll admit. I see secrets you're afraid to share. I see the love you've yet to confess. Sometimes I almost think I see the past. . . .

"No! Don't close your eyes," he cautioned as she tried to avoid his all too perceptive scrutiny. "Don't put that wall between us. I'll tear it down, Bri. That's a promise. When I come back, I don't want anything keeping us apart. I want all of you. All of you," he stressed, rubbing his fingers in tantalizing circles against her soft skin. "And I'm not going to settle for stolen kisses on a public beach."

"No fair," she whispered as the spiral of familiar sensations began to build. "I can't even think—"

"Don't think, Bri. Just feel," he begged, his voice no louder than a prayer. "Just love me."

She stiffened in his arms but didn't say a word.

Strong fingers tensed along her waist.

"It's too soon," she protested. "You're not free. Please don't push. I feel guilty enough."

His breath left him slowly, in a long frustrated sigh. Just as slowly he eased himself away from her. "You neglected to mention we're in a very public place," he pointed out.

"And I should get back to Noah. Luke's been with him all morning," she explained.

The look he leveled on her was stoic and shuttered. But she saw the pain disguised behind it and regretted mentioning Luke. "I'm sorry," she said softly. "I didn't—"

"Shhh, Bri. Let's not start on that again. In a way I'm grateful Luke's given us this time together." He tugged her closer as he spoke. "Kiss me good-bye?"

As he enfolded her in his arms, the wariness dissipated. She felt comforted and secure. She relaxed, leaning against him for support. His fingers were gentle, toying with her hair and then tracing intricate patterns along her spine. For those few moments she was transported backward in time. She didn't move for fear she would break the magic of the moment.

"I'd like to hold you like this all night," he whispered. His lips brushed her temple.

Shivers of delight surged through her as his warmth met the flesh on her neck. She ached for him to claim her lips. But he was in no hurry. It seemed to be ages later when his mouth began the journey slowly across her jaw, tentatively capturing her mouth and lingering while he explored its shape.

The fire inside Brianna began to burn out of control. She pressed her lips insistently against his, asking, taking all she could. But she wanted more than kisses. She wanted all of him. She longed to wrap herself around him, to share the completeness that had been lost to them for so long. A soft moan escaped, coming from the depths of her soul.

"You know," he whispered as he rained light kisses onto her eyes and nose, "we've got . . . this backward. We keep meeting . . . intimately . . . in very public places."

His words brought her all too swiftly back to reality. "Oh, Jess," she moaned. "You make me forget there's a world outside your arms."

"But there is. And we need to return to it." He cradled her chin in his hands and gazed into her eyes. "I guess this is good-bye for a while." His voice sounded strange, choked with emotion. "You understand why I need to leave?"

"Yes, of course," she murmured.

"I'm not sure I could go if you didn't, Brianna," he admitted. "This is one of those thorns I have to touch."

"I know, Jess." She stroked his cheek, wishing he would either kiss her again or just leave and be done with it. "I want this behind us, too."

"When I come back, the rules will have changed," he reminded her.

She nodded and moved to step away, but he detained her with a kiss she would not soon forget.

"Go," he commanded when he released her. "And tell Luke thanks for baby-sitting."

He left her then. Instead of going back to the cottage, she watched him jog along the breaking water. Watched until she lost sight of him.

*At least he said good-bye this time,* she thought as the physical warmth of his farewell kiss began to fade. Nothing would dim the emotional heat he'd spawned. Nothing ever had. Not time. Not distance. Not even doubts.

He said he'd be back. Perhaps he would. Perhaps this time they had a future. He'd said, "Just us." But she knew it could never be the two of them alone. Her world included Noah. If and when he came back, she'd have to find a way to tell him about their son.

She knew it wouldn't be easy. But he had to be told. He'd said he trusted her. God, she hoped he did. Their present relationship was new, fragile, untried.

Five years ago she could have told him anything

without fear of misunderstanding or recrimination. But today, after the pain of abandonment and separation she'd experienced, after the wrenching emotional and physical blow he'd been dealt, she wondered how she could possibly find words that could lessen the shock for him.

He had always expected honesty. It was one of the traits she admired most in him. Now it had become something to avoid.

And family, she thought woefully. Although he'd mentioned his brothers occasionally, the only family they'd ever spoken of was theirs—the family their love would create. She'd known he wanted children, but she hadn't known how all-important family was to him. They'd loved each other as if no one else mattered, as if nothing outside their world mattered.

She had learned the hard way that others did matter. . . .

And now, partly because of others, she was afraid to tell him about their own precious son. Now she understood what family meant to him. And she couldn't bear to inflict any more wounds onto his already scarred soul.

But she had her own reasons, too.

What had he said just before he left? "This is one of those thorns I have to touch."

*Oh Jess,* she wailed silently, *this rose is covered with thorns.*

# TEN

Jess MacLaren knocked twice on the front door of the weathered little cottage. No one answered. Feeling frustration well up inside, he started to return to his car, then, as an afterthought, trudged toward the beach behind the cottage. His efforts were rewarded.

Not far from the back door a large blanket was spread out over the hot sand. Brianna sat there, idly sifting the fine white grains through her fingers. A cascade of sable hair fell across her face, shielding her delicate features from his scrutiny. But right now he didn't care that he couldn't see her face. He stood rigid, drinking in the sight of her, thankful he had found her at home.

Then he drew in a deep breath and crossed the sand, his eyes glued to the woman he loved. When he spoke, the deep timbre of his voice shook with reverence. "Brianna" was all he said.

Her head came up abruptly. The eyes that lifted to meet his adoring gaze were alive with surprise. "What are you doing here?"

"I wanted to see you." He reached to gather her in his arms. His need for her all but consumed him. He trailed soft kisses along the smooth ivory flesh of her forehead and the side of her face, then moved on to the warmth of her lips, claiming them with an urgency that would not be denied. Yet he needed more. His hands slid possessively down her back, urging her ever closer.

"We shouldn't be doing this, Jess, not here," Brianna cautioned as she attempted to move from the intimate enclosure of his powerful arms.

"You asked what I was doing here. This is why I'm here. I had to hold you and taste you," he murmured, bowing his head for more. His hands moved artfully, searching and massaging the tight muscles in her back. His mouth captured hers again, seeking its sweetness.

"I couldn't leave without saying good-bye properly," he explained. "Sara had a baby girl late last night. Luke's already gone. He caught a flight home early this morning." His fingers found their way into her silken tresses, crushing the luxurious sable to his palms. He hugged her closer and inhaled the mildly fragrant scent that lingered on her. Satisfaction washed over him in sweeping waves.

"I had to see you. I couldn't think about anything but—" Distracted, he stopped short. Near the water's edge a small dark-haired boy frolicked, splashing gleefully.

Brianna's son, he realized. As he watched the child drag a plastic pail through the sand to a lopsided sand castle, his hold on Brianna slackened. His hands dropped to his side. Every muscle in his body tensed while Noah painstakingly poured water into a makeshift moat.

Without conscious thought he stepped away from her and moved toward the child, his gaze fixed on the profile of the boy's sun-warmed face.

The profile was familiar. He'd seen it before. Often. In his brothers. In his cousins.

He dropped into the sand, afraid his suddenly unsteady legs would collapse beneath him. His eyes darted over Noah again and again.

*Sweet Lord, he's mine,* he swore silently. And then echoes of previous conversations traveled through his mind. "WHERE'S YOUR SON'S FATHER? . . ." "He doesn't know he has a son. Fate never gave me the opportunity to tell him. . . ." "DID YOU LOVE HIS FATHER VERY MUCH? . . ." "Yes. Now and always . . ." "IF HE WALKED INTO YOUR LIFE AGAIN, DO YOU HONESTLY BELIEVE YOU'D LOVE HIM AS MUCH? . . ." "I'd love him more. I know I would . . ." "HOW OLD IS HE, BRIANNA? . . ." "He's four. . . ." "YOU KNEW ME BEFORE, DIDN'T YOU? . . ." "Yes . . ."

He shut his eyes and inhaled the damp sea air, gradually filling his lungs, hoping it would help calm the rapid thundering of his pulse in his ears. And when he was certain he could breathe without willing his body to do so, he opened his eyes and fastened them on Noah again.

*He's mine! No wonder she trembles when I push her too hard. How I must have hurt her. Did I love her? Damn, if only I could remember. None of this would have happened. Brianna bearing our child alone. Alone. She wasn't much more than a kid herself. It must have been hell. . . .*

Remorse and an inexpressible amazement assailed him one after the other. The sound of Noah's giggles of delight filled him with wonder. On another level he heard the waves breaking on the beach and the gulls sweeping through the sky above. But all he saw was Noah. His child. A stranger . . .

Deep inside other emotions began to build, then churn wildly out of control. He struggled to keep the spiraling intensity at bay, but with each passing moment, the new emotions grew stronger.

His son. A dark-haired miniature of the man he faced each time he looked in the mirror. Noah's cap of thick, sable hair was the only noticeable difference.

He rose to his feet, unaware of the dampness in his clothes and the sand clinging to his legs.

She watched his mechanical movements, sensing that he had recognized Noah. Her stomach knotted in apprehension. This was the moment she'd longed for and the moment she'd dreaded ever since he walked back into her life. All she could manage to do was wait nervously and hope he would understand.

She glanced at Noah, then back at Jess. The eyes that met hers were filled with questions. Her heartbeat seemed to thunder in her ears. When he called her name, she started, then moved slowly forward. Before she closed the gap between them, his control shattered.

"You didn't understand anything I said yesterday, did you?" he charged. "You couldn't have." His words were clipped, biting. "No one can imagine how it feels. The hell. The desperation. Confusion. Time lost . . .

"It's awful not to be able to remember," he groaned in frustration. "I can't remember . . . I just can't remember. No matter how much I want to. No matter how hard I try. I can't remember."

"Jess—"

"You don't understand," he accused, silencing her

with a glare. "It's only a year. Yet it's a lifetime. *My* lifetime." He glanced toward Noah and nodded. "*Noah's* lifetime." His eyes came swiftly back to Brianna.

"Memory's a strange thing. We take it for granted. What you did yesterday or the day before or last year, you carry along with you. Then, pow! You wake up and your little brother is fourteen and three inches taller than he was . . . yesterday. And your sister's married, but yesterday she wasn't even engaged.

"Then a stranger in a white lab coat tells you— kindly, in hushed tones—'You've been in a car accident. You may be disoriented.'"

"Disoriented," he bit out. "Disoriented," he repeated, shaking his head. "It's much more than that. I had a huge hole cut out of my memory, a piece of my life ripped from me, taken away. It's gone! Like essential sections of a puzzle purposely destroyed." He swallowed hard, fighting back the flood of emotions that had been unleashed.

"And everyone's older. Mom's grayer. Dad's thinner, almost gaunt. Luke's grown a mustache. Drew has a full beard. Sara's married. Rachel's matured physically, but she hovers next to me with a sort of haunted look in her eyes. And Ethan isn't a little dark-haired kid anymore." Jess shot an assessing look at Noah.

"Confusion," he whispered, sighing as the memories continued. "Then more heaped on top. Explanations of an accident I hope I *never* remember. And slowly a realization. I'm missing more than the few unconscious weeks spent in a coma.

"Sara carries a wedding picture in her wallet. I'm in the bridal party. Mom shows me an album filled with pictures of family events I've been part of but don't remember.''

He clenched his fists and scowled at the injustice and then at Brianna as she opened her mouth to interrupt a second time.

"Let me finish," he commanded. "I want you to understand. Fully understand . . . I hated the feeling of helplessness then, Brianna. I had to force myself to go forward. Looking backward was painful because of the missing time—and for reasons I still can't explain to anyone.

"I hated it!" he reiterated. "But my family pulled me through. Literally. Dad insisted if he could get up and go on after his heart attack, then I couldn't sit back and quit. And Rachel . . . begged me to be the brother she remembered.''

He closed his eyes, envisioning his sister's tear-ravaged face. "She thought she'd lost both Dad and me. She wanted her family to be the way they'd always been. She said she needed my strength. . . .

"So I took control of my life—again. I went forward.'' His eyes found hers and held them fast. "I refused to look back," he explained solemnly. "It hurt too much. Every time I weakened and let my mind veer off its course, I was tormented all over again.

"Maybe torment seems like a strange choice of words, but I can't think of any other. It wasn't a physical torment. Neither was it simply mental anguish. Kind of a hell, a limbo in between.

"After I met Chris, we were always on the go. Concerts, theater, family gatherings. No time to wonder what I used to do. I fooled myself into believing the healing process was complete.''

He stared at Brianna, amazed by her fragile beauty,

yet puzzled by the complexities of the human mind that prevented him from seeing as far back as he wanted.

"And then, you were lying in my arms. Soft, beautiful, bewitching." He paused, remembering the confusion in her expression and the feel of her sweet, warm lips pressing against his own.

He closed his eyes to recapture the visual memory.

"Jess?" she whispered, reaching out to touch his shoulder lightly.

"Your eyes enchant me," he murmured. "Before that day in Boston, I'd never seen eyes so pale and yet so blue. Except . . . in my dreams . . ."

"Luke persuaded me to come back here. I agreed because I knew I couldn't go forward anymore. I needed to find the missing pieces of my life.

"And here you are." He searched her face. "The beautiful stranger who fainted in my arms. The blue-eyed enchantress who bewitches me with her soft voice and warm kisses." His fingers traced the delicate curve of her cheekbone, then trailed downward to cup her chin. "Are you the key?" he challenged softly.

Brianna shook her head. "You said yourself, memory is a strange thing. How can either of us know if I'm the key to your forgotten year?"

"You know things about me you won't share," he accused. "Considering what I *thought* was happening between us, that only increases the confusion. I've been more open with you than with anyone outside my family. I've told you things I haven't told Chris in the two years we've been together. I've tried to explain my frustrations to you . . . but it's clear you didn't understand."

"But I did. I do," she insisted.

"No," he countered. "No, you don't, Brianna. God, I hate lies and deceit!"

"I haven't lied to you—"

"Nor have you been altogether truthful. You've neglected to divulge things that are critically important to me." He spoke deliberately and with quiet emphasis. His eyes remained riveted on Brianna, entreating her to understand and to respond.

"Tell me about Noah," he demanded suddenly. "I want to know everything, what he likes to eat, what he likes to play, what his favorite toys are, what's in that collection of 'neat stuff' you've told me about. . . . Everything about him."

"He likes to eat pizza and ice cream," Brianna began. Then she paused to take a deep breath, as if it were necessary. She glanced fleetingly at him, but her eyes seemed to seek out her son.

"He loves to play in water, especially the ocean, as you can see. Little cars, most anything with wheels, are his favorite toys. He loves to look at books and listen to stories. . . . You don't honestly want to know what's in his collection, do you?" she asked, her voice heavy with disbelief.

"Tell me everything," he repeated, "everything, Bri. Down to the last pebble in his collection."

"Oh, Jess," she moaned, clenching and unclenching her fingers at her side. She longed to reach for him, but she sensed an emotional gulf between them even though they stood within touching distance.

"Noah's collection is a hodgepodge of the stuff every little boy loves, but it's his, uniquely his own. I can close my eyes and see his face shining with the delight of discovery each time he finds a special something he considers worthy enough to add to it. There are shells we collected at the beach—clams, scallops, oysters, mussels. And stones he's picked up as we've taken walks. Sticks he's gathered in the woods and kept because he thinks they look like a gun or a sword. And string—ratty pieces of string—colored yarn, twine, some old buttons. A silver crayon, and a gold and copper crayon, too. A couple of stickers that won't ever stick to anything again. And broken pieces of colored plastic—the green is his favorite. Some acorns and chestnuts, a couple of grapefruit seeds . . .'' Her voice grew fainter as she spoke.

"This isn't easy for either of us, Brianna." He recognized her distress. It was not difficult to read her emotions. She was shaking, and as he studied every detail of her face, probing deep into places only he could see, he witnessed her inner battle, too.

Yet he offered no help. He made no move to touch her. Anger and frustration overruled his compassionate side.

"I need to hear you tell me . . ." He paused just long enough to feast his eyes on Noah, drawing strength from that simple action. Then he waited impatiently for the words he desperately longed to hear.

She knew what he wanted, knew the time had come to admit the truth to him, but she'd never imagined it would be so difficult. And she'd never wanted to tell him like this—with Noah so close by. Drawing on her inner strength to see her through, she squared her shoulders and raised her eyes. But when she tried to speak, she faltered, then choked on the words. "Noah . . . is . . . your son."

"*Our* son," he corrected. "*Our* son. Why didn't you tell me?" he pleaded. "I'm his father, Brianna. Doesn't that mean anything? Doesn't family mean anything? Don't you think a father has a right to know?"

"I meant to tell you, Jess—"

"When?" All at once his control snapped, unleashing the anger. "Were you planning to send me a graduation announcement? When, Brianna? He's four! You've had plenty of time."

"I didn't know where you were."

"You've known for nearly two months! You've had weeks to tell me! Why the hell didn't you know where I was?" he queried as her reply sank in.

He watched her blink back tears, then raise her chin in defense. But he was so consumed by his own emotions that her stoic actions barely registered.

"I went to your apartment, but you weren't there," she explained. "No one could tell me anything."

He nodded once. "Pretty flimsy excuse. And when you found me in Boston you decided to keep my son a secret?"

"No," she denied in a rush. "I was waiting for the right time."

"The right time?" he scoffed. "You've had two months!"

"I didn't want this to happen," she stressed, reaching out to him. "I didn't want you to be hurt."

He stepped back, keeping her at arm's length, avoiding her touch. "Oh hell, Brianna. Do you expect me to believe that?"

"It's the truth," she declared. "I wanted to find a way to tell you—"

"How could I be so gullible?" He sliced one hand through the air to halt the flow of words. "How could I let you deceive me—"

"I didn't. I haven't," she insisted vehemently. "Please listen, Jess. Please try to understand."

"Understand? You didn't bother to tell me I have a four-year-old son. All the times we talked about him. All the times I told you I wanted children." He glared at Brianna. "You had plenty of opportunity to say something," he reminded her. "Frankly I can't begin to understand why you didn't!"

"How could I?" she protested. "How do you tell a stranger he's the father of your son?"

"But you knew me!" he countered. "Unless you shared a stranger's bed five years ago?"

Brianna closed her eyes and prayed for the strength to see this through. Prayed that Noah wouldn't grow curious. Prayed that the noise of the surf would muffle their raised voices.

She pressed her quivering lips together and drew in a slow, steadying breath. One of them had to remain calm and clearheaded. Somehow she had to be that one.

"No," she finally answered him. "I loved you. We weren't strangers. We were lovers." Her voice was quiet but strong. "I've never stopped loving you, Jess. I love your son, too. And I won't let *anyone* or *anything* hurt him. Ever."

She paused, dramatically. When she spoke again, her voice was colored with a determination he'd never heard before.

"That includes you, Jess MacLaren. Noah had nothing to do with what happened then, and I'll do anything I have to do to see he doesn't get hurt now."

"I'm his father. I won't hurt him," he insisted.

"Maybe not intentionally."

He reached out and grabbed her shoulders, digging

his fingers into her flesh. "You're the one keeping him from his family."

Brianna winced, as if he'd raised his hand to her. "I've given him what family I can—"

"Don't fathers count?" he interrupted, enunciating each word. And then the brilliance of sunlight caught in the sparkling diamond on her left hand.

He glared at the ring, admitting to himself for the first time how much he hated the sight of silver circling her finger.

"What happened, Brianna? Did you run to another man for comfort? Did he dump you when he learned you were pregnant?"

Her mouth dropped open in surprise. "No," she was quick to deny. "No, Jess. Please listen. We were engaged. You and I."

"No more lies, Brianna—"

"That's the truth!" she interrupted.

"The truth? You expect me to believe we were engaged? In five years no one's said a word about a fiancée. Don't you think that's odd?"

She nodded, biting her lip. "I'm sure you think so. I guess you didn't tell anyone. Our relationship was very private—"

"Private," he echoed harshly. "We slept together."

Her eyes filled with pain. She swallowed hard, then continued. "Believe what you like. I'm telling the truth," she insisted, her voice quiet but firm. "We were lovers. We kept to ourselves. You gave me this ring the last time I saw you—"

"Right," he scoffed. "You expect me to believe I asked you to marry me and you'd never met any of my family? And why the hell didn't you look for me?" he thundered suddenly. "If, as you tell me, we were engaged, why the hell didn't you show up after the accident?''

"I couldn't find you," she explained. "You didn't meet me as you'd promised. You weren't at your apartment. No one I talked to knew where you'd gone."

"You didn't call Steve at the office?"

"I didn't know Steve. The only phone number I had was to the apartment. There was no listing in Lewes for Jess MacLaren. I tried," she stressed.

He shook his head wearily. "What I believe is that you've tried to keep the truth from me. And you've kept my son from me."

"Would you like me to introduce you?" she asked.

Her question took him by surprise, not only the words, but the bold look in her eyes and the challenge in her posture. "Oh, that's rich, Brianna. Keep him a secret for weeks, then, when I'm standing here blazing mad cause you've successfully deceived me all this time, offer to introduce me. As if I hadn't hinted often enough."

"Jess, I—"

"No." His grip tightened. He shook her once and, regretting his action, willed himself to relax, smoothing his unsteady hands down her back. "Not now. Children are much more perceptive than we realize. I will not have him thinking an angry, irrational stranger is his father."

"But—" she tried to protest.

"You put me off, begging me for time," he reminded her. "Now, as much as I want to scoop him into my arms and hold on to him, I'll wait. I need time to cool down, to regain control, and to incorporate the idea of immediate fatherhood into my life."

He forced himself to release her, lowering his hands to his sides as he took a quick step away. "Time," he muttered, balling his fingers into tight fists. "And distance. So I can think rationally again. But I'll be back," he promised, glancing toward his son for one last look.

The image of Noah splashing in the water stayed with him long after he'd walked away.

The heavy wooden door slammed into the wall as Jess stormed into Luke's room. "Why the hell didn't you tell me?" he bellowed. "You knew. Dammit! Why didn't you tell me?"

Luke, who was bent over his drawing board, looked up at his brother and scowled in confusion. He made an elaborate show of putting his work aside and setting his pencil down.

"For a moment I thought you were Drew, busting through my door like that. Exactly what are you demanding, anyway?"

"Noah," he ground out. "You knew about Noah!"

Luke blew out a breath of air that ruffled the hair over his eyes. "Guilty as charged, counselor," he admitted, holding up his hand when his brother tried to interrupt. "I didn't tell you because it wasn't my place. That responsibility was Brianna's—and hers alone. I take it she told you?" he asked, cocking his head to one side.

"No dammit. I saw him."

"Oh, hell," Luke swore. "No wonder you're so angry." He rolled his eyes toward the ceiling. "Did you blow up at her or did you save that for me?"

"This isn't funny, Luke. She kept my son from me."

"Not without reason," Luke tried to explain.

"Reason! What possible reason can there be for denying a father his son?"

"Just look at yourself," Luke countered. "You dare ask why she couldn't tell you? I doubt if she's ever seen you angry. You're always in control. Apparently your son's mother knows you very well. And cares about you. She anticipated your reaction. She didn't want you hurt or raging—and now you're both."

"Make me understand, Luke," he begged. "All I can see is black and white. Honesty and deceit. Brianna deceived me. She kept my son from me—but not from you!"

"Hey, back off. I'm just the baby-sitter. What she tried to keep you from was hurt. And she was afraid, too. Afraid you wouldn't understand. Afraid you'd try to take Noah. She'll do whatever she has to do to protect him. She told me he's her life."

"The reason she makes it through each day, each crisis she faces . . ." Mac said, remembering Brianna's words and the look she'd had in her eyes. He remembered she'd expressed similar thoughts earlier in the day when he'd confronted her.

He sank onto Luke's bed and rested his head in hands. "I turned my back and walked away."

"From Brianna?" Luke questioned.

He nodded twice.

"Way to go, big brother," he muttered. "Little boy's games. She hurt you. You hurt her back."

"Oh hell!" Mac rasped. "I didn't mean to hurt her. I wasn't thinking. I just reacted. I was outraged. Indignant. How could she keep him from me? How dare she?"

"And how dare you?" Luke interrupted.

"How dare I what?" he asked, puzzled.

"Not see her side," Luke said. "Where's the rational, levelheaded lawyer? Two sides to every case, big brother," he reminded him.

"Her side," Mac said thoughtfully.

"Yeah. She was young. You disappeared. She

couldn't have had an easy time. She was alone. But she came through, made a life for herself—and for your son," Luke emphasized quietly. He hitched himself up on the dresser top, dangling his long legs. "Then she found you. But you didn't know her. Now I imagine that's a little hard to buy."

"But *now* she knows what my family means to me. Why didn't she tell me?"

"Mac, she's thought it through, carefully, thoroughly. She's not just afraid to hurt you or have you hurt Noah. She loves you, you know. She's willing to risk hurt for herself, I think, but she's cautious, real cautious."

"She hadn't said she loved me—" he broke off. Again her earlier words rang in his head. This morning she had confessed her love for him—and for his son.

"Have you told her how you feel? How do you feel, anyway?" Luke asked, grinning.

Mac raised his eyes to Luke. "Before I found out about Noah, I told her I loved her."

"And now?" Luke challenged.

"I love her," he admitted quietly.

"But?"

"I feel deceived . . . And disappointed."

"Believe me, big brother, Brianna would never intentionally deceive anyone. She was feeling desperate, backed into a corner. She was, in fact, trying to find a way to tell you without hurting you." Luke paused, fixing an odd, pleading look on his brother. "Give her a chance."

He nodded once, then again. "One drunk driver," he muttered.

"Yeah," Luke drawled.

"I shook her. I actually shook her," he confessed, his voice raw with emotion.

"That was dumb. She's been hurt enough."

He exhaled loudly. "I know. But I don't know how to begin to work this out."

"Try one step at a time. A heartfelt *I'm sorry*, followed by *I love you*." Luke tried to make light of the situation.

"Followed by *Will you please do me the honor?*"

"Brianna called that one," Luke mumbled.

"What?" Mac's head snapped up. "What did you say?"

"Brianna knew you'd insist on doing the right thing. Which is another reason she didn't tell you that you're a daddy. She doesn't think strangers make good lifetime partners."

"We're not strangers anymore. Apparently we weren't strangers five years ago either. We were engaged. Did she tell you anything?"

"If you have relationship questions, you should ask Brianna," Luke advised, turning to dig through the small chest on top of his dresser.

"Do you think she'll forgive me?"

"For exploding?" Luke queried. "Yeah. I think she'll understand."

"God. What do I do if she says no?" he worried out loud.

"She'll forgive you. Don't worry."

"I meant to marriage. I need . . ." he trailed off.

"Maybe this will help," Luke suggested. His fingers curled round the object he'd been searching for. "Okay, listen up. Once upon a time about five years ago, I found something that didn't belong to me. It belonged to you, Mac, but you were . . . not quite yourself," he paused, remembering. "While you were in the hospital, unconscious, Drew and I made a hasty trip to Eaton. We packed your stuff to bring home."

Jess MacLaren met his brother's eyes. Luke appeared agitated and remorseful at the same time. "Must have been hard on both of you."

"Yeah," Luke agreed. "But it had to be done." He sucked in a large breath and shook his head. "Anyway, while Drew was out picking up lunch, I found this . . . treasure.

"I want you to understand a few things. You know I don't keep secrets from you. I would've given this to you long before if I had thought it could help you remember." Luke looked straight at his brother. "But I figured it would be excess baggage, adding to your frustration. I never thought the time was right."

He slid off the dresser and extended a small velvet box toward Mac. "You might like to have this now."

Mac's questioning eyes darted rapidly back and forth between his brother and the box. At last he reached out, taking it gingerly from Luke's hand. The seconds crept by with agonizing slowness while he raised the lid. Silence filled the air as he stared down at the box, then removed the piece of paper that was tucked inside.

Luke sat back on the dresser, waiting.

Mac's gaze finally shifted from the paper to Luke. Long moments passed before he revealed his thoughts.

"According to this piece of evidence," he tapped the jeweler's receipt in his hand against the ring box, "Brianna's telling the truth. I must have asked her to marry me," he murmured. "And . . . I must have loved her."

# ELEVEN

Brianna stood silently by Noah's bedside, watching her beloved son. Like all children, Noah looked angelic as he slept, and she couldn't resist the urge to touch him. She pulled a light cover up to his shoulders and, for the second time that night, carefully tucked it around him, pausing to gaze at his sleep-warmed face and stroke his little cheeks ever so gently. Then, sighing in the darkness, she turned to leave the room.

Jess was standing in the doorway, his tall frame silhouetted by the light from the living room.

"How did you get in?" she whispered.

"I let myself in. You should remember to lock your door at night," he scolded.

"Hmm." She nodded. "I was preoccupied."

"With Noah?"

She shook her head. "With Noah's father."

He sighed, then swallowed so hard she heard him. Intense green eyes, shadowed in the dim light, stared down at her.

"I'm sorry, Brianna. Deeply sorry. I don't see how I can ever make all this up to you."

He extended his hand and laced her fingers with his, then tugged gently, drawing her close to him. His free hand rose to her face, touching her suddenly too warm flesh with unmistakable reverence.

"I know I owe you one hell of an apology. I knew that before I came here tonight. But then I saw you with Noah." He drew in a great breath of air. "And I realized how much love you've given him . . . and me. In that moment I realized how powerful love is. And I knew no matter what lay before us, we'd face it— together. No matter what obstacles the Fates throw in our pathway now, we'll be strong enough to override any and all of them as long as we do it together.

"But it'll take me just about forever to apologize for all the times you've faced alone . . . and for the things I said to you, not to mention storming out the way I did—"

"You were hurt, Jess," she said. "You needed time to reconcile past and present."

"Right this minute I need to kiss you," he murmured as his head bowed to capture her lips.

His kiss was the sweetest possible apology, wrapped up in a promise, linking all that had passed between them and all that was to come.

"Let's go into the other room," he suggested, his voice heavy with emotion. "We'll be more comfortable and we need to talk."

For a fleeting instant he was concerned she would refuse to talk again. But she followed him without hesitation. And as he stretched out on the couch and patted the space next to him, she joined him, snuggling close, as if it were second nature.

"You've already forgiven me, haven't you?" he asked, unconsciously stroking the silken cascade that fell onto his shirt.

She sighed and toyed with his buttons, one at a time, avoiding his eyes. But as she lay against the broad wall of his chest, comforted by the touch of his fingers in her hair, an old feeling of contentment came over her. She realized he was waiting for an answer. She walked her fingers along his abdomen, thankful for the freedom to touch him again.

"Didn't you mention something about forgiving me a thousand times?"

"I did," he remembered. "Your eyes lure me into some fathomless abyss. Each time I'm drawn in is like the first. But this is different. I hurt you, Brianna. First I left you alone and pregnant. And you forgave me, didn't you? You must have," he continued, not waiting for her answer, "because when you kissed me in front of half the population of Boston, what I felt then was unencumbered, uninhibited."

He nudged her chin toward him with one gentle finger and was at once lured by the tender emotions he read in her eyes and the soft smile she bestowed on him.

"I loved you five years ago. I loved you that day in Boston. I love you now . . . and I'll love you for always."

"Even though I hurt you again? Even though I doubted you? Accused you? Even though I turned my back?"

"I have an advantage, Jess," she explained quietly. "I know how much you loved me before. I know how strong our love was. And deep down inside lives a glimmer of hope that you'll somehow feel that way

again. You said watching me with Noah made you realize how powerful love is. I already know that.'' Her
voice was as gentle as a caress.

"I never wanted you just to happen upon Noah like
you did, Jess. I wanted to tell you myself." She bit her
lip to hold back tears. "I couldn't find a way because I
knew how very hurt you'd be. . . . And you were. All
I saw then was your hurt. I knew your words were
fueled by it, and by anger and frustration. As much as
I love you, I couldn't prevent that. I can't blame you
for venting your anger.

"Watching you walk away was harder than listening
to any of the accusations you'd hurled at me. It tore
me apart. If I hadn't had Noah to hold on to, I don't
know what I would have done.

"I didn't know if you'd be back. I couldn't think
beyond the moment. Every time I closed my eyes I saw
you walking away. And each time I remembered how
it felt the first time. I was so afraid. I didn't know if
you were going back to Boston to talk with Chris, or
to see Sara's new baby, or to distance yourself from
me.

"I kept telling myself you'd come back. You said
you would. And I knew you'd have to see Noah. . . ."
She glanced at him and grimaced. "Your anger filled
me with doubts. But I understood, Jess. There wasn't
anything to forgive."

"Plenty to forget, though?" he suggested.

"My time with you has always been precious," she
told him. "When we were younger, it was stolen hours
before you went to your office each morning. Occasionally an evening, if you weren't swamped with work."
Her voice shook with emotion as she remembered.

"And the time we've spent together since then has felt like borrowed time."

She searched his eyes, seeking understanding. And when he lifted her hand and pressed his lips to her palm, she saw the reassurance she needed.

"It's not borrowed, Bri. Not anymore. This is our time. Yours and mine. And Noah's," he insisted.

"Fate, in the guise of a drunk, may have torn us apart five years ago, baby, but those seemingly cruel Fates kindly brought us back together. You came to Boston because of your book, Bri," he emphasized. "And the book was an indirect result of the love we shared. The attraction I couldn't explain or ignore was our love drawing me back to you . . . and to our son."

His words reached out to her. His intense look held her captive, not only physically, but emotionally and spiritually as well. Yet it was more than the manner in which he was speaking and the wealth of emotion she found in his eyes. She heard more than spoken words. She heard the love and the sincerity in his voice. And she saw her future in the depths of his eyes.

"Brianna, I know it couldn't have been easy for you." He faltered, searching for the right words. As he inhaled the fragrance that meant heaven to him, a warmth of emotion pulsed through him and a knot of tension tightened his throat. He swallowed hard, knowing he had to press onward, had to ask questions. He didn't want this gulf between them, yet he was hesitant to open old wounds or cause her pain, even remembered pain.

"I know you don't like to discuss having Noah . . . but I have no way of knowing what happened. Will you tell me?"

Although she could see love written plainly on his

face, he was asking her to remember the pain and the scars time had healed. And without knowing, he was asking her to lay open wounds inflicted by her once secure, now shattered family.

Silently she acknowledged the time had come to talk, to unburden herself, to share the inner secrets with him. She turned nervously in his arms, stretching out her small hand, symbolically giving him her trust before she tore open the long-healed wounds.

She talked for over an hour, filling him in on the details of her life after he disappeared. She touched lightly on her summer vacations in Eaton, glossed over her parents' volatile reaction to their teenage daughter's pregnancy, and praised her sister for giving her a home.

For the most part Jess listened in silence. He groaned when he realized she'd been only eighteen. He interrupted again to clarify her parents' position. Her explanation was uncharacteristically blunt. She'd left their home in deference to their attitude. She had not returned.

Several times he murmured an apologetic "Bri, I'm so sorry." But always he maintained a comforting hold on her. And when she was finished, they sat wrapped in silence, both thankful to put the past truly behind them.

As he kept her secure in his arms, he struggled with his conscience. Brianna's explanation weighed heavily on him. So much that had impacted her life had happened because of him and because of the accident.

"I love you so much, Brianna. And I owe you so much. . . . More than time, more than years. What I owe can't be measured or repaid. All the days and nights you've faced alone with Noah, all the love you've given him . . . And all the thorns along the way. I'm responsible for creating your lonely road."

"No, Jess," she denied quickly. "No. You weren't the cause. We were equally responsible. Noah was created through our love."

"Through our love," he echoed. Twining her hand in his, he pressed one finger against her ring. "Wish I remembered . . ."

"Don't, Jess. Don't put yourself through anymore."

"I'm okay, Bri," he assured her. "You know that baby-sitter of yours, the one with the mustache? He's a good guy. Helped me get my act together. I've always relied on logic, sought explanations for everything. The accident turned my world topsy-turvy. This damn amnesia obscures so much I'd like to know—especially about us.

"I should have relied on my instincts. Followed them. Believed in you and what you seemed to be. I hope you understand what I'm trying to say."

"If you're trying to apologize again, it isn't necessary," she said softly.

"It's necessary, Bri. My frustration, my emotions, overwhelmed me. I took it out on you. I didn't get control until Luke showed me the receipt for the ring."

"He knew?" Her eyes widened in surprise.

Jess smiled. "He didn't tell you either?"

She shook her head and he gave her a quick, affectionate squeeze. "He did all he could to bring us together without actually interfering, didn't he?"

"He did," she whispered.

"How do you thank someone for giving a piece of your life back?"

She smiled up at him. "In this case, that's easy. He loves Noah—" she broke off.

"And I love Noah's mom," he murmured, rubbing his index finger lightly across her bottom lip. The gesture drew Brianna's full attention. His finger moved slowly to the base of her chin, tilting it so that short of closing her eyes, she could not avoid his intense, probing stare.

"Brianna, will you marry me?"

"Because of Noah?" she whispered. "I don't want you to feel obligated to marry me because of something that happened five years ago. Noah and I—"

"Hush, Bri, hush," he instructed, covering her mouth with his own to ensure her silence. For long, sweet moments he held her lips captive, sliding his own over hers, tasting her, and wanting much more than the touch of her mouth beneath his.

"Yes, because of Noah," he eventually answered. "Because I want our son to be part of a real 'mom and dad' type family. Because I want the very best, the happiest life for him a child can have. And because I want him to know the love of both his parents. I want him to have brothers and sisters, and maybe even a dog. All of those reasons, Bri, but also, because I love you, and I want you to share my life, all my tomorrows."

Compelled to draw her even closer, he slid his hands along her back until his fingers hugged the gentle curve of her hip. Then he cradled her intimately against himself and pressed her so close he could feel her heart beating rapidly next to his. And as he gazed into her eyes, he saw beyond the moment. Once again he bowed his head, powerless to resist the feel of her sweet lips.

While he kissed her, he searched for her left hand. And when he found it, he stroked the slender band of silver, whispering softly in her ear, "I love you now.

And I must have loved you then.'' He lifted her hand to his mouth, planting kisses on her palm. "This ring is my proof.''

"But so much has happened—''

"Did any of it change your love?''

"No,'' she declared. "Nothing ever will.''

"No,'' he repeated. "This ring is a symbol of our love. And even though we didn't exchange any formal vows, it bound you to me, Brianna.''

"I don't expect you to fulfill a promise you don't remember,'' she stressed.

"How about a promise I want to make now? I love you,'' he insisted. "I want to hold you in my arms each night, watch you wake each morning. . . .'' His voice, heavy with emotion, caught and he paused briefly before continuing. "I want you to share your laughter, your anger, your fears . . . and your love.''

She listened to his words but heard much more than words. She heard the intensity of his feelings, the longing, and she heard the love. She considered these things, weighed them thoughtfully. "Please be sure, Jess.''

"I am sure'' was his confident response. He bent his head to kiss her tenderly and to affirm his statement in a way he was certain she would understand. "I'm quite sure,'' he murmured as his mouth brushed against her parted lips once more.

"What about your forgotten past?''

"I've given it a great deal of thought, Bri, more than anyone knows. I live with this dilemma daily. Keeping my distance, giving you the time you asked for, was difficult. Pretending there's nothing between us didn't work. It made me realize how eager I am to begin building a future, *our future*,'' he stressed. "If it's meant to be, the past will come back to me. It will all fall into place. And that's the reality I have to accept in order to go forward.

"Will you marry me, Bri?" he asked again.

"Yes, Jess," she consented quietly. "I'll marry you. I couldn't very well refuse after that speech."

"Can I hold you in my arms until tomorrow, or are you going to send me away tonight?"

"I need you here, Jess," she replied. "I don't want to sleep alone."

"Nor do I, Brianna," he confessed. "Not ever again, baby." He brought her hand to his lips, kissing each slender finger deliberately. His magnetic eyes held hers captive as his mouth delivered a series of slow kisses to her palm and then continued advancing along the soft flesh of her inner arm.

She was engulfed by the inevitable weakening his touch spawned. Each gentle kiss increased her awareness. While her thought processes slowed, her emotional needs begged to be acknowledged.

Pale blue eyes, filled with longing, communicated silently with his. Their message could not be misinterpreted.

At first he simply held her next to his heart, as if she truly were a china figurine. But he needed more than the feel of her warmth against him. He pressed his starving lips against her mouth, seeking the emotional nourishment only she could provide.

For a time the only reality was the sweetness of their kiss. But his gentle touch and hungry kisses created sensations within Brianna that had long been denied. Flashes of heat and desire rushed through her. While his mouth continued its intoxicating plunder of her lips and face, his hands raced insistently up and down her spine, sending shooting currents of uncontrollable desire through her.

The electricity his touch generated chased all thought from her mind. Time stopped. Her senses gained complete control. She wrapped her arms around his waist and molded her body closer to his, communicating the urgency of her own growing need.

And then suddenly his control vanished, too. He could wait no longer. Moaning in pleasure, he swept Brianna into his arms and carried her to bed. With their mouths still locked together, they fell onto the mattress. He rolled, gently placing Brianna on top of the bedspread, stretching out alongside her.

He read the silent consent in her bright eyes and knew she wanted and needed as much as he. As he eased the sundress from her shoulders and lowered the fabric to unclothe her breasts, he realized he needed this woman as much as he needed air to breathe. For endless seconds, he studied her, fascinated by the woman and by his overpowering feelings. Desire-filled eyes caressed her. And then his head bowed to shower soft, wet kisses over her exposed flesh. When he captured the taut peak of her breast with his marauding mouth, he felt her writhe beneath him in ecstasy.

Driven by this sensual onslaught, Brianna longed for the feel of his bare skin against her own. She tried to pull back to coax Jess away, yet at first neither could part for even a fraction of a second. Gradually and with exceptional effort, she made a space between them. And then she was able to touch his shirt, able to reach out, with dreamlike movements, to remove his clothing. Her slender fingers worked deftly to unfasten one button at a time. Slowly she uncovered the firm wall of his chest, then tentatively began to explore it with her hands.

When he was free of his shirt, when she finally tugged it off his shoulders and tossed it onto the floor beside the bed, it was as if, with shedding that item of clothing, she had also shed her reserve.

Her caresses grew increasingly bold. She ran her fingers through the thick, russet hair on his chest, touching him without restraint—at long last feeling his flesh beneath her fingers again. Her hands inched upward along his broad shoulders, down the length of his muscled arms, then across the width of his back, gently kneading and searching as she reacquainted herself with every inch of the magnificent body she had never forgotten. She reveled in a feeling of renewal, a feeling akin to coming home.

The unexpected demand in Brianna's touch surprised him, and he felt a deep, compelling need to become part of her that grew stronger with each moment of sensual contact. His eager lips sought hers, taking them in a deliberate, mind-drugging kiss. His hands traveled along her hips tantalizing, and at the same time searching. Eventually he grabbed on to the thin fabric that was the final barrier between them. In one masterful effort, he removed it.

Then he paused to simply feast his eyes on the delicately formed woman. Her lips begged him to taste them again, and he was helpless to deny their silent request.

Brianna lay beside him, not only naked and exposed, but totally enraptured by the power of his persuasive mouth and the provocative movement of his fingers on her sensitive flesh. She grew more and more frantic to feel his skin against hers. When she clutched at his belt buckle trying inexpertly to release it, he seemed to understand the intensity of her need.

Without saying a word he helped her unfasten his jeans. Just before her hand closed round him, he remembered to retrieve the small foil packet to protect her.

And when that was accomplished, when heated flesh rubbed against heated flesh, his eyes found hers, acknowledging their mutual need, acknowledging the inevitability of the next moment.

Time fell away. Weeks, months, years didn't matter. Only love. Only sharing that love. Brianna and Jess were consumed by the golden wave of passion that flowed between them, and over them, and swept through them like the incessant tides of the sea. And finally, the lovers were reunited in a gesture as timeless as the tides.

A soft thud from the bedroom drew Brianna's attention from the kitchen sink, and she turned abruptly. "He's awake, Jess."

"Good," he responded, sighing. "I'm ready whenever you are. We need to get acquainted." His eyes sought hers. "I don't know him at all, Bri. I don't know what makes him laugh, or what makes him angry. Or if he's more like you, or more like I am, or if he's a blend of both of us . . ."

She moved toward him and was, at once, wrapped in his arms. His mouth covered hers greedily. She sensed renewed confidence in his touch and in his kiss this morning, as if their commitment to each other and their night together had erased the years between.

"Ready." She smiled up at him, then called to her young son. Jess felt her tense beneath his fingers.

"It'll be all right," he assured her. "He's mine. I love him already."

"I know, Jess. But—"

He pressed her closer, soothing her with yet another kiss, this one more potent, more passionate than the previous gesture.

A few feet away, wide green eyes watched in fascination.

"Why're you kissing my mama?" Noah's innocent voice interrupted his parents' exchange.

Brianna felt Jess's smile against her lips, felt, too, the chuckle that rumbled in his chest.

As he shifted, turning slightly, he found himself captured by Noah's wide eyes.

"I like kissing your mama," he explained to the curious little boy.

Noah held his gaze, his little eyebrows wrinkled as he stared hard. "You have green eyes like my Uncle Luke, only different. Uncle Luke takes me fishing," Noah boasted.

"He does, huh? He's really something," Jess mused, making a mental note to thank Luke. "Your Uncle Luke is my brother. Sometimes brothers look alike. All my brothers have green eyes."

"Do you have lots of brothers? I told Mama and Uncle Luke I wanted a brother. Mama said she couldn't promise. I think that means no," he said, disappointment obvious in his voice.

Jess searched the child's face, understanding coming naturally to him. "I promise you'll have lots of brothers, Noah."

"Honest? Oh boy!" Noah exclaimed happily. "Mama, he says I can have lots of brothers!"

Brianna leaned against Jess, relieved. She had longed

for this moment for years and now she knew the wait was over. As she watched, tucking away this scene to remember forever, she was deeply touched by Jess's loving acceptance of his small son.

"Sometimes you have to wait a while for brothers," Jess explained to Noah. "We'll see what we can do."

"Okay," he bobbed his head up and down. "What's you name?"

"My name is Jess MacLaren."

Small, dark eyebrows wrinkled again. For a minute he stood wordlessly, with a half-puzzled look on his face. "Jess . . ." he said at last. "Mama talks to you when she's sleeping. I heard her. Her eyes were shut, but she was talking."

Jess smiled broadly. "I imagine I talk to your mama when I'm sleeping, too."

"That's dumb," Noah remarked.

Chuckling again, he nodded his head in agreement.

"Mama says you're her friend."

"I am," he admitted.

"Uncle Luke told me about girlfriends. Is Mama your girlfriend?"

"She is," he answered truthfully.

"Does that mean you love my mama?" Noah asked.

"Yes, Noah," Jess responded, "I love your mama very much."

"Yeah," Noah drawled in a perfect imitation of his Uncle Luke. "But Uncle Luke doesn't kiss Mama same as you."

"That's probably because your mama isn't Uncle Luke's girlfriend," he said. "She's more like a sister. Understand?"

"Guess so," the child responded agreeably. His wide eyes kept returning to stare curiously at his mother.

Jess couldn't help but notice. He sighed then and, temporarily relinquishing possession of Brianna, raked his fingers through his thick hair.

"Jess?" Brianna queried softly.

"Bri," he whispered so only she could hear, "trust me? We're going to be married and I'm going to be daddy, agreed?"

She stood on tiptoe to place an approving kiss on his cheek. "Agreed."

"Why do you call Mama Bri?" Noah asked curiously. "That's not her name."

"Jess has always called me Bri, kind of like Uncle Luke calls you sport."

"Always?" Jess questioned.

"Just about. And no one else ever has," she answered. "You wanted to discuss something important with Noah, didn't you?" she reminded him.

"You'll have to help," he murmured, reaching toward the little child to lift him into his arms. "This will be our first family discussion." He sat down in a kitchen chair and settled a wiggly Noah in his lap, then turned to Brianna. One brief, reassuring glance at her, and he faced his son.

"Do you know what married means?"

"Aunt Laura and Uncle Tom are married," Noah replied.

"That's right, they are," he agreed. "Married means they went to church and had a special service. They made some important promises to one another so they'll always be a family. Do you understand that?"

"What kind of promises?" the boy wanted to know.

"Oh, things like always loving one another, no matter what. And staying together, even when things go wrong," he told Noah. But he was watching Brianna, already making those promises with his eyes and with his heart.

"Are we a family, Mama?"

"Yes, Noah," Jess answered for her. "We're a family."

Noah looked confused. "Are you married, like you said?"

"Not yet, but soon we will be. In a few days we'll go to the church in town to be married. You can come along with us."

"And that'll make us married like Aunt Laura and Uncle Tom and Jenna and little Tommy?" Noah wanted to know.

"Almost," Jess explained patiently. "We have to sign some grown-up papers, too, Noah, so your mama and you can have the same name as I do. Then we'll be a family exactly like Jenna's family."

"We're not 'zactly like them. Jenna has a mommy and a daddy—" Noah began.

"And so do you," Brianna stated quietly. "Jess is your daddy."

The child stared up at his father's face. "You told me my daddy has green eyes, Mama. Is he my for real daddy, or just pretend like in storybooks?"

The intense expression on Noah's face, which mirrored Jess's earlier expression, brought forth a wave of overwhelming joy. "He's your for real daddy," she replied in a voice that was merely a whisper.

Although he seemed to accept this information easily enough, Noah was not quite satisfied. "But we still aren't a family 'zactly like Jenna! She has a baby Tommy, too."

Jess began to laugh out loud, but Brianna's look

stopped him. "Didn't I promise you lots of brothers, Noah?" he reminded his son.

"Yeah, just like you said you have," Noah remembered excitedly.

"Maybe not that many," Brianna protested.

Suddenly Noah asked, "What's my name gonna be? You said we'd have the same name as you."

Jess's eyes caught and held Brianna's for a brief moment. Then he smiled warmly at his son, "Noah Dugan MacLaren."

The bright look on the child's face faded.

"What's wrong, Noah?" Brianna asked.

"I thought my name was gonna be Jess, like his," he replied, sulking. "Baby Tommy has the same name as his daddy."

Jess tightened his hold on Noah. Witnessing the child's disappointment was difficult. "Don't you suppose we'd get awfully confused if your mama called for Jess and we didn't know which one of us should answer? Why don't you be Noah and I'll be Dad?"

"Can I call you Dad?" he asked timidly. His eyes widened with wonder. Some of the former excitement returned to his face.

"Yes, Noah, I'd like very much if you called me Dad," he remarked huskily.

Noah turned and wound his small arms as far around Jess as he could to hug him. Happily returning the hug, Jess held his son tightly in his arms. He felt Brianna's fingertips as she reached to touch both of them lovingly while they embraced. And when he glanced toward her, he found her pale eyes were glowing with happiness.

Jess grinned like a silly child as they pulled into the driveway of the MacLaren home in Boston. Brianna had remarked on his odd behavior several times earlier in the day. When he turned off the car, she couldn't resist the urge to tease him again.

"You're still wearing that ridiculous grin, Jess," she stated, her eyes sparkling with amusement.

"I can't help it, Bri," he sighed. "I suppose it's ecstasy and anticipation all rolled into one. Come on, let's go," he encouraged, the enthusiasm written in his face echoed in his voice.

Noah scrambled out of the backseat of the car, immediately gripping his father's large hand.

"Is this where we're gonna live?" he asked. His eyes were round as saucers as he stared at the huge house.

"No," Jess replied. "This is where I lived when I was a little boy. We're going to live in my town house until Mama and I find our own special home. All right?"

"Okay," Noah agreed amicably. "Who lives here?"

"Uncle Luke does," Jess told him, possessively wrapping his free arm around Brianna. "And your Grandma and Grandpa, and Uncle Ethan and Aunt Rachel live here, too."

"Wow!" Noah exclaimed. "That's why it's so big."

Jess chuckled. "I suppose it is."

Brianna's grip tightened as they climbed the steps to the front door.

Jess paused momentarily to reassure his wife. Cheerful malachite eyes collided with anxious azure blue.

"I love you, Bri," he vowed, his voice filled with reverence. "My family loves you, too. Ready?" His eyebrows arched in question as he reached for the doorknob.

He allowed Brianna to enter, then followed. Noah

was the last one in. He slammed the heavy door shut, causing Jess to roll his eyes heavenward.

'I suppose whoever is home knows we're here now,'' he laughed, turning toward Noah to ruffle his thick hair.

Seconds later Libby MacLaren's gentle voice had him turning to face her.

"Brianna, it's wonderful to see you again,'' Libby said, folding her into a warm embrace and making her feel instantly welcome. "And my son, the big oaf, tells me congratulations are in order.''

"Hi, Mom,'' Jess said, reaching toward his mother for a hug.

"Hi, yourself,'' she grumbled good-naturedly. "I'm mad at you, Jess MacLaren. Calling me *after* the wedding! What a shock! You've always been so predictable—''

"We have another surprise, Mom,'' Jess informed her, grinning that silly, excited grin he'd worn all morning. "This little fellow hiding behind me, acting shy for the first time in his life, is Noah.''

Mrs. MacLaren stepped away from her son to welcome Noah. Her mouth dropped open, then promptly closed.

"Look at you!'' she exclaimed in a voice no louder than a whisper. "Come over here and give Grandma a hug, Noah.''

Brianna held her breath for a fraction of a second, but there was no need. Noah literally bounced forward into his grandmother's open arms, returning her affectionate squeeze wholeheartedly.

"I have a surprise, too,'' she smiled as she stared in amazement at her grandson. "Why don't you come along with me, Noah, and we'll introduce your mom to your brand new baby cousin?''

Noah took her hand without hesitation and started to follow, then stopped suddenly.

"Mama's crying," he said, sounding very concerned.

Libby MacLaren raised her eyes from the child to his mother. "Sometimes," she explained as she caught a glimpse of her eldest son drawing his wife into a comforting embrace, "adults cry, Noah. Especially when they're very happy. I suspect that's why your mama's crying. Why don't we go check on Megan and let your dad and mom have a few minutes alone?"

"Okay," the child agreed hesitantly, but he trotted willingly by her side as they left the room.

Several minutes later Jess and Brianna joined them in the den, where the baby was napping.

"Mama, look how little she is!" Noah exclaimed in a loud whisper. "Grandma said not to wake her. We're s'posed to whisper," he explained.

Brianna nodded, smiling at her young son.

"Hard to believe she's that tiny. Her mother looked like she was going to have twins," Jess commented as they all stared down at the sleeping infant.

"She's beautiful," Brianna breathed. "She has such delicate features."

"She's gorgeous," Jess agreed. "Like her mother."

"Hmm," Brianna murmured.

"Are you all right, Mom?" Jess queried suddenly, releasing his possessive hold on Brianna. "Those are tears of happiness?"

"Yes," she responded, accepting the comforting hug her oldest son offered. "Complete happiness." She reached out to include Brianna in their embrace. "He's beautiful," she whispered.

"I know," Brianna agreed softly. "I've always thought so, too."

"Well, well, well." Sara's lilting voice sounded from the doorway. "Look who's here. My rotten brother, the one who got married without inviting his family to the wedding!"

"He invited family," a young voice contradicted.

Sara's emerald eyes sparkled as she moved gracefully into the room "He did?" she challenged the little boy she saw standing next to the bassinet.

"Yeah," he drawled in a perfect imitation of his Uncle Luke. "I was at the wedding, and Uncle Luke and Aunt Laura and Uncle Tom."

Sara raised her hands in surrender. "Okay, okay. So he had a family wedding." She shook her head at the child. "He forgot to invite *me*," she complained. "I'm his sister! And who might you be?" she inquired, staring into eyes every bit as green as her own.

"Noah Dugan—" he began, stealing a quick peek at his father, who nodded once before the child continued. "Noah Dugan MacLaren," he finished proudly.

Sara beamed at the little boy. "I'm your Aunt Sara and this is Uncle Ted." She swept her arm through the air to indicate the smiling blond-haired man standing behind her. "And that tiny little baby is my very own precious daughter," she announced.

"I know," Noah acknowledged. "Grandma told me."

"Well? What do you think of her?" Sara challenged.

"She's awful small, but she'll grow. Baby Tommy's getting bigger. He can crawl now."

"Baby Tommy?" Sara's lovely face looked decidedly curious.

"My sister's son," Brianna explained.

"Oh," Sara nodded. "Welcome to our family, Brianna," she said, bestowing a brilliant smile on Brianna as she moved to embrace her. "You are going to stay with us longer this time, aren't you?" she dared to tease.

"Definitely," Jess responded. "This visit is permanent."

"I'm glad," Sara smiled.

"Uncle Luke!" Noah yelled, forgetting the sleeping baby.

"Whoa! Slow down, sport!" Luke cautioned, lifting the large box he held in his hands just as Noah propelled himself into him.

"Hi, all!" Luke greeted them collectively. "Saw your car outside, big brother. I thought this might be a good time to give you your wedding present. The sooner, the better. Wait, sport," he instructed Noah, who was practically bouncing with enthusiasm.

"I'm certain Mac and Noah are gonna love this gift," Luke continued, "but I forgot to check with you, Brianna." He sent her an apologetic look. "Come on, Noah. Let's go sit down with your dad and your mama. All three of you can open the box at the same time."

Gleefully, Noah obeyed, skipping toward the sofa, then plopping down on his father's lap.

"No speeches," Luke remarked, handing the large box to Brianna. "You two know how I feel. I thought this was the perfect gift for a family."

Brianna raised the lid of the box quite slowly.

"Hurry, Mama," Noah chirped.

"Oh, Luke," Brianna breathed. "How beautiful!"

"Oh boy! Wow!" Noah exclaimed.

Jess reached around his exuberant son, gently extracting a wiggly Irish setter puppy from the box. The entire family witnessed the recurrent silly grin. "She's perfect, Luke," he remarked, holding the puppy for all to see. "Perfect. Thanks."

"Yeah. You're welcome," Luke acknowledged. "What do you think, Brianna?"

Tears had filled Brianna's eyes, but she smiled happily at her brother-in-law. "I have to agree with Jess. She is perfect," she revealed softly. "When I was a child, we had an Irish setter. I always loved that dog. . . ."

Jess leaned toward her, planting a light kiss on her forehead. "We'll love this one, too, Bri," he grinned. "Perhaps we'd better let our little *girl* outside for a romp in the yard," he suggested.

'Yeah," Luke agreed. "It's been a while. Good idea."

"Come on, Noah," Jess urged, grabbing on to the child's hand. "Let's show the new addition to our family the backyard."

And with that the trio left the room.

# EPILOGUE

The early morning sunshine kissed the beach of the all but deserted cove. Jess MacLaren strode purposefully over the sand toward the place where he knew his wife would be waiting. Noah skipped along beside him, chattering at his usual fast clip.

Suddenly the child let go of his hand and dashed away toward the breaking waves. Jess chuckled softly to himself as he watched Noah frolic at the water's edge. Their relationship had developed easily from the beginning and seemed to deepen with each passing day. It still bothered him to remember the years he hadn't been able to share. But he was thankful Noah seemed to be forgetting there had ever been a time in his life without his dad.

Jess took a deep breath of salty ocean air and felt his chest puff up with pride as he studied his small son. And then he lifted his gaze to the wide beach beneath the dunes, searching for his wife.

She was there. A delicately diminutive china doll, sitting alone, waiting for him as she had in the past.

*Déjà vu*, he thought, closing his eyes. When he opened them and looked again, he froze, staring sightlessly in Brianna's direction. Brief flashes of past experiences were exposed in his mind's eye—remembrances of early morning rendezvous and late night lovers' trysts assailed him.

*I loved her*, he remembered. His eyes fastened on her tiny dark-haired form, he began to move swiftly, jogging to close the expanse of sand between them. And when he was several feet away from her, he stopped and stared in wonder.

"Jess?" she inquired, puzzled by the odd look in his eyes and the unusual crooked smile on his face.

"Hi, blue eyes!" he finally exclaimed. "Seems I owe you an explanation. Mom called to tell me Dad had a heart attack and was in the hospital." He continued as if six years had not passed. "I got ready to leave for Boston as quickly as possible. It was late at night, and I meant to call you from home in the morning. . . ." Bending to kneel in front of her, he said half apologetically, "I never made it home, Bri."

"I know. Luke and Mom filled in the important spaces for me," she explained. "When did you remember?"

"Only moments ago," he murmured. "Moments ago as I saw you sitting alone on the blanket. I knew I'd seen you like that before. . . ."

"What else do you remember?" she questioned, tilting her head to one side as she peered up at him.

"Snatches. All I've got are fuzzy little pieces. But you, Brianna, are part of each fuzzy piece. You and those lovely blue eyes . . . And Bethany has them, too," he added, looking down at the tiny child whose pale blue eyes had closed while she nursed contentedly at her mother's breast.

As he crouched in the sand next to them, Jess lifted his hand to Brianna's face, staring reverently. "I've always been drawn into your eyes, Bri. From the first time I saw you here on the beach, your lovely eyes have enchanted me. And that day in Boston, as you woke up from your faint, I remember thinking your exquisite eyes were like the ones in my dreams."

He laughed softly, then dropped to sit on her blanket, leaning back on his elbows and stretching out his long legs. He expelled a long, relaxed breath, his eyes moving over Brianna, openly caressing every inch of her.

"I feel terrific! I remember, Bri. I loved you! You were right to believe me. I meant every word I said. I never, willingly, would have been able to walk away and leave you behind. I never meant to leave without saying good-bye. . . . I remember buying your engagement ring, planning to bring you champagne and roses and the ring. But I couldn't wait. I wanted to see it on your finger. You were then, and always will be, a special part, the most important part of my life." He ran his hand playfully up over her spine and under the cascade of long hair to her neck. Then shifting his weight to one side, he extended his arm and drew her to him.

"Our love, Brianna, was strong enough to endure time, and distance, and barriers. Our paths were always meant to cross. You were the restlessness within my soul, the reason I felt incomplete after the accident, the past I was missing and needed to find so desperately. And now that I have you, there's not much more I could want."

He leaned toward her, hungrily capturing her lips

with his own, keeping her as close as he dared without harming their baby daughter. As their embrace ended, he lifted the sleeping child from Brianna's arms, then cradled her safely against his chest.

"I missed this with Noah. I don't want to miss any part of their lives, Bri." He paused, momentarily suspended in thought, remembering pieces of yesterday.

"We've come a long way, blue eyes. In the past fifteen months we've progressed from two strangers thrown together by some odd quirk of fate, to friends uncertain of past and future and fighting both, to what we are today. Incredibly lucky married lovers."

He drew a finger ever so lightly across the baby's soft auburn hair. "All that we are to each other, Bri, and for each other, is because we've found ourselves in finding each other."

"Two halves of a whole," she murmured.

He smiled as he gazed at his wife. It was a brilliant, radiant smile. "I feel complete, Bri. I can't remember feeling so complete, so whole, before in my life."

"I've always felt that way with you," she revealed softly.

"I remember holding you, when I shouldn't have been holding you, and thinking how right it felt," he confessed. "And earlier, as I watched you in the distance, *knowing* I'd seen you there before . . . I felt whole again, for the first time in years. And when I realized how much I loved you six years ago, I realized what treasures I've found . . . reclaimed. The three of you are precious treasures—worth touching all the thorns along our lonely paths."

"Oh Jess," she murmured.

He almost didn't hear her over the constant lapping

of the waves. But he saw his own strong emotions reflected in her eyes.

As the space between Brianna and Jess dissolved, no spoken words were necessary. The lovers' kiss said it all.

Their fate was sealed.

of its waves. But to-day, loaded down, straining
onward in her race.

As the quivering, flaming car has blossomed so
sudden with new garden. The towns that still to

Then they will reach

## SHARE THE FUN . . .
## SHARE YOUR NEW-FOUND TREASURE!!

You don't want to let your new books out of your sight? That's okay. Your friends can get their own. Order below.

### No. 143 HEAVENLY by Carol Bogolin
Men like David were the ultimate temptation and Kathlyn vowed to resist!

### No. 144 OUTSIDE THE RULES by Linda Hughes
Jamie and Stephen play a dangerous game with high stakes and no rules.

### No. 145 UNTIL TOMORROW by Sandra Steffen
Bekka wanted to know the truth about Conor but he wasn't about to tell.

### No. 146 PRIM AND IMPROPER by Rachel Vincer
Julia couldn't make Martin understand there could be no truce—no way!

### No. 147 HANNAH'S HERO by Denise Richards
Kane was dead! Either Hannah was losing her mind or he *was* alive.

### No. 148 ANYTHING YOU CAN DO by Sara Garrett
The More Bailey fought Austin, the more he wanted to win her heart.

### No. 149 VOICE IN THE DARK by Judy Whitten
Rae finally faced the man who saved her life. Now can she save his?

### No. 150 NEVER SAY GOODBYE by Suzanne McMinn
Felicia had achieved all of her dreams . . . except for one—Brandon!

--------------------------------------------

**Meteor Publishing Corporation**
Dept. 693, P. O. Box 41820, Philadelphia, PA 19101-9828

Please send the books I've indicated below. Check or money order (U.S. Dollars only)—no cash, stamps or C.O.D.s (PA residents, add 6% sales tax). I am enclosing $2.95 plus 75¢ handling fee for *each* book ordered.

**Total Amount Enclosed: $_____.**

| ___ No. 156 | ___ No. 133 | ___ No. 139 | ___ No. 145 |
| ___ No. 128 | ___ No. 134 | ___ No. 140 | ___ No. 146 |
| ___ No. 129 | ___ No. 135 | ___ No. 141 | ___ No. 147 |
| ___ No. 130 | ___ No. 136 | ___ No. 142 | ___ No. 148 |
| ___ No. 131 | ___ No. 137 | ___ No. 143 | ___ No. 149 |
| ___ No. 132 | ___ No. 138 | ___ No. 144 | ___ No. 150 |

*Please Print:*
Name _____

Address _____ Apt. No. _____

City/State _____ Zip _____

Allow four to six weeks for delivery. Quantities limited.